***"Axel Clay, what are you doing here?"***

Tara didn't sound welcoming and wished she didn't care.

"We need to talk."

"After four months of silence? I don't think so." *Darn it. That didn't sound indifferent, either.*

"Tara—"

He's just a guy, she told herself for about the millionth time since that night in Braden had turned into an entire weekend. More than forty-eight hours spent with each other in that little motel room, during which she'd started thinking things she'd had no business thinking. Crazy things. Forever things.

All of which had come to a screeching halt when he'd been gone before she'd woken up the last morning. The only thing he'd left behind was a note that he'd "call."

Well, no call ever came. All they had in common was one weekend…and an unborn baby that she needed to keep secret….

Dear Reader,

I started reading romance novels as a teenager. I particularly liked Harlequin and Silhouette Books. Not only were they affordable on my babysitting income, but they were plentiful and I didn't have to hide them from my mother! Not until I was an adult, though, did I dream that I could write one of those books that I so loved to read.

Now, it's a decade since my first book, *Stay…*, was published, introducing Jefferson Clay and his family. I'm still astonished at the reception they've received. I am incredibly honored that so many of you have loved them and continue to want more! Together, we've even moved on to the next generation of the family, and it seems particularly remarkable to me that Jefferson's son, Axel, was chosen to be part of the FAMOUS FAMILIES collection.

So thank you for the moments we've shared. I treasure them all.

Best,

*Allison*

ALLISON LEIGH

# A Weaver Wedding

Silhouette®
SPECIAL EDITION®
Published by Silhouette Books
**America's Publisher of Contemporary Romance**

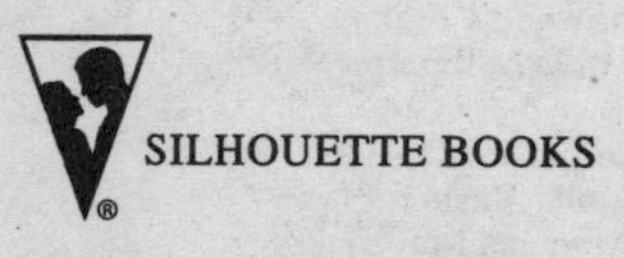

ISBN-13: 978-0-373-65447-5
ISBN-10: 0-373-65447-2

A WEAVER WEDDING



This edition published by arrangement with Harlequin Books S.A.



Visit Silhouette Books at www.eHarlequin.com

**Printed in U.S.A.**

**Books by Allison Leigh**

Silhouette Special Edition

†*Stay...* #1170
†*The Rancher and the Redhead* #1212
†*A Wedding for Maggie* #1241
†*A Child for Christmas* #1290
*Millionaire's Instant Baby* #1312
†*Married to a Stranger* #1336
*Mother in a Moment* #1367
*Her Unforgettable Fiancé* #1381
*The Princess and the Duke* #1465
*Montana Lawman* #1497
*Hard Choices* #1561
*Secretly Married* #1591
*Home on the Ranch* #1633
*The Truth About the Tycoon* #1651
*All He Ever Wanted* #1664
*The Tycoon's Marriage Bid* #1707
*A Montana Homecoming* #1718
‡*Mergers & Matrimony* #1761
*Just Friends?* #1810
†*Sarah and the Sheriff* #1819
†*Wed in Wyoming* #1833
****A Cowboy Under Her Tree** #1869
††*The Bride and the Bargain* #1882
**The Boss's Christmas Proposal* #1940
§*Valentine's Fortune* #1951
§*A Weaver Wedding* #1965

†Men of the Double-C Ranch
‡Family Business
**Montana Mavericks: Striking It Rich
††The Hunt for Cinderella
*Back in Business
§Fortunes of Texas: Return to Red Rock

---

## *ALLISON LEIGH*

started early by writing a Halloween play that her grade-school class performed. Since then, though her tastes have changed, her love for reading has not. And her writing appetite simply grows more voracious by the day.

She has been a finalist for the RITA® Award and the Holt Medallion. However, the true highlights of her day as a writer are when she receives word from a reader that they laughed, cried or lost a night of sleep while reading one of her books.

Born in Southern California, Allison has lived in several different cities in four different states. She has been, at one time or another, a cosmetologist, a computer programmer and a secretary. She has recently begun writing full-time after spending nearly a decade as an administrative assistant for a busy neighborhood church, and currently makes her home in Arizona with her family. She loves to hear from her readers, who can write to her at P.O. Box 40772, Mesa, AZ 85274-0772.

For everyone who has loved
The Double-C family as much as I have.

## *Prologue*

"Can I get you another margarita?"

Tara Browning looked up into the sympathetic eyes of the cocktail waitress as she moved the empty glasses from Tara's table to the tray balanced on her palm.

Wasn't there a rule somewhere that drinking alone was a bad sign of something?

Beyond the waitress, the wood and leather-studded Suds-n-Grill was just about standing-room only. Maybe that meant Tara wasn't alone, even if she *had* been stood up by her own brother. She forced a smile. "Sure."

"Have it out in a few minutes." The waitress disappeared among the bodies crowded into the small bar.

Tara sighed and glanced over the people. Still no sign of Sloan.

She couldn't pretend she wasn't disappointed. The message that her twin brother had left on her phone had been the first time she'd even heard his voice in three years. Five since she'd seen him in person and turned her life upside down because of the choices he'd made in *his* life.

She should have known he wouldn't show, despite his message. Not even on this, their thirtieth birthday.

She exhaled and accidentally caught the eye of a middle-aged guy staring at her from his seat at the bar. She looked away. She wasn't looking for a pickup. Occupying bar stools wasn't something she indulged in even in Weaver, where she lived and worked, much less here in Braden, a good thirty miles away. She'd come for Sloan McCray. Period.

"Do you mind if I take the extra stool?" The kid from the overflowing, high-top table next to hers was eyeing her earnestly over the top of his longneck beer bottle.

She shrugged. It wasn't as if she needed to save the seat for Sloan. "Go ahead."

The kid slid the stool three feet to the other table. "Thanks, ma'am."

*Ma'am.*

Happy big fat three-oh to you, Tara.

The guy at the bar was still eyeing her and she turned slightly on her stool, accepting the fresh margarita from the waitress. She didn't know why she'd bothered ordering any drinks when she had no head for alcohol. Nor did she know why she stayed in the crowded bar at all when it seemed painfully clear that her brother wasn't going to show, no matter what his message had said.

She pushed off the stool, swaying a little dizzily. She wasn't about to hire a cab to take her back to Weaver. Even if she could find one, she'd have to turn around and make the return trip in the morning to retrieve her car.

Which meant a night in the motel across the highway.

If she'd stuck to drinking lemonade, she could have driven right back to Weaver where she belonged.

The irony of that thought didn't escape her.

She didn't belong in Weaver, either.

The story of her life.

"Heading out already?"

She stopped short when the shape in her path took form, but realized immediately that it wasn't the middle-aged man who'd been eyeing her. No. This guy was tall and blond and definitely not portly.

She peered up at him, focusing with an effort. His head topped her measly five feet four inches by about a foot. Even in the dim light of the crowded bar, his eyes were a startling golden brown. "Axel? Axel Clay?"

The man pressed a wide, square palm against his chest. "So, you do remember me." His sculpted lips tilted. "I'm touched."

It was hard not to remember. The Clay family was pretty much the bedrock of Weaver. The men were all one version or another of tall and ridiculously handsome, and the women were as varied and as beautiful as flowers growing wild in the fields. A Weaver resident would have to live under a rock not to recognize one of them.

"What are you doing here?"

He grinned a little, lifting the squat glass he held. "Wetting my whistle like everyone else."

"I meant in Braden." Her brain felt fuzzy. And he smelled way too good. Amid the crush of bodies in the bar, he seemed like a haven of crisp, fresh air. A magnificently, beautifully, male haven. "You haven't been around Weaver for more than year." She flushed. "At least, that's what I've heard in my shop."

He caught Tara's elbow and nudged her out of the way, allowing another cocktail waitress to pass. "I've been out of the country."

She'd heard that talk, too. His frequent travels; his talent for horse breeding; his status as a thoroughly eligible—albeit uncatchable—male.

He smiled at her and her head swam. Maybe that's what

she got for living the life of a nun, even at the ripe old age of thirty. She had a drink, saw a handsome man, and had to battle against a tidal wave of unfamiliar desire.

"So, how's business at Classic Charms?"

She moistened her lips, wishing that she hadn't abandoned her drink back on the table. Holding it would have given her restless hands something to do, other than tremble with the ridiculous urge to feel if his hair was as thick as it looked. "I'm surprised you remember the name of my shop." He'd been there only a few times, usually accompanying his mother.

His lips tilted again. "Hey now." His golden gaze dropped for a moment to her mouth. "You're not the only one with a memory. I remember all sorts of things."

She felt more parched than ever. "Business is good. I'll have to hire a part-timer, soon. Before the holidays."

"You still have that old phone booth in the center of the store?"

She blinked. "Uh, yes." The vibrant red phone booth was currently housing a display of not-entirely-innocent lingerie that she'd gotten at an estate sale.

He dashed his fingertip down her nose. "Told you I remember things." He tossed back the rest of his drink. "So, what are *you* doing here in Braden?"

She barely kept herself from touching her tingling nose. "I was supposed to meet my brother here. But he…he couldn't make it."

He covered her shoulder with his hand and she went still before realizing he was merely moving her aside again for another passing waitress. "His loss is my gain. Let's grab a table."

She was unbearably tempted, though she tried not to be. "I don't think there are any left." The one she'd abandoned had already been claimed.

"Then, we'll dance." Before she could protest, he'd grabbed her hand and led her to the crowded, minuscule dance floor.

Digging in her heels did no good. She was caught in his storm surge, and that was all there was to it. Then he was turning her into his arms and she felt like she was going under for the last time.

"I don't dance," she warned, having to practically yell to be heard over the loud music. Jukebox. No live DJ or band for the Suds-n-Grill.

He settled her left hand on his shoulder and took her waist. "All beautiful women dance."

She was a far cry from beautiful, but whether it was his words or his hand on her waist, she felt fresh heat streaming from her face to her toes. Delectably filling in every nook and cranny along the way.

The music pulsed around them while some rumbling-voiced singer lamented unfulfilled desires. She could feel the imprint of every one of Axel's fingertips against her waist, right through her tomato-red tunic. Maybe it was her imagination that those fingertips seemed to subtly flex against her, like the sheathed claws of some big, golden cat kneading against his soft prey.

She'd lived in Weaver for five years. But she'd never gotten personally involved with anyone there. Hadn't gotten involved with anyone even before that. Not since her brief, unsuccessful marriage about a million years ago.

Somewhere inside her dim brain, she remembered that a dance did not qualify as involvement. She moistened her dry lips. "You, um, you didn't come here to meet someone?"

His head angled toward her and his voice seemed to whisper over her ear. "I got stood up, too."

"Who would stand *you* up?" The words came without thought, and her face went hot all over again.

His lips tilted. "At the moment, I'm having a hard time remembering because I didn't expect to enjoy myself at all. And yet—" he said as he drew her closer "—here we are."

Her head swirled again, only this time it wasn't the least bit unpleasant.

And those fingertips of his were pressing more insistently into her waist. His thumb, where their hands were joined, slowly dragged across her palm.

Liquid fire drenched her veins. He might as well have pressed his mouth against hers she was so transfixed.

"It's my birthday," she said stupidly.

His gaze was steady on her face. That faint, not really amused, quirk still on his sculpted lips. "Did you blow out the candles and make a wish?"

She'd had a wish. To see the only family she had left for the first time in too many years. Given the fact that she had no way of reaching Sloan—he'd left *her* the surprising message—she'd thought that was something her brother had wanted, too. Now she knew better.

"No cake," she told Axel. "No candles."

His thumb slid down her palm again. "Ah, now, that just ain't right. Birthdays always come with a cake and candles where my family is concerned."

She wasn't surprised. There wasn't a soul who lived in Weaver who could be unaware of what a tight-knit clan the Clays were. From all appearances, his family was the complete antithesis of hers.

"When it's just one of you, cake and candles leem a snittle—" she explained, then frowned and marshaled her tongue with some deliberation "—seem a little unnecessary."

"Well, it's not just one of you tonight, anymore." His gaze became even more hooded. His thumb wasn't stroking any longer. It was situated, dead center, against her palm where it felt as if an electric current was passing directly through to her heart. He turned his head slightly as if he was studying their hands pressed together, and her blood seemed to rush to her head. "Feels like there're two of us to me," he murmured.

Her heart bounced around. Her skin felt tight, her nerve endings wanting suddenly to burst free. "Okay." The word came out more like a breath, but his mouth still slid into a slow, satisfied curve.

He linked his fingers through hers and before she knew it, she felt the cold rush of October night air across her hot face as he pulled her right out the front door.

It vaguely dawned on her that she'd forgotten her jacket, but then it didn't matter because there, just out of the light of the entrance, he slid his arms around her shoulders, turned her boldly into his arms, and covered her mouth with his.

Sensation blasted through her with all the warmth of a summer afternoon and her head fell back, her mouth opening beneath his.

His hand—oh, it was so warm, so gentle, so strong—covered the base of her neck. Slowly slid along her throat until it reached her jaw.

"Dude. Get a room." A laughing male voice said from behind them, followed by a trill of female giggles.

Axel lifted his head, but he didn't even look back at the snickering couple entering the bar behind them. His gaze stayed on her face, but his hand cradled her throat where she felt certain he could feel her thundering pulse. "Wishes aside for the moment, what do you *want* for your birthday, Tara Browning?"

She moistened her lips and tasted him on them. "You." The word escaped. Bald. Husky. The blush that hit her face was scorching. "Sorry. Blame that on the margaritas."

"I was hoping *I* had something to do with it." His fingers splayed against her spine, and he nudged her even closer until not even Wyoming cold could get between them.

She inhaled. Everywhere that she was soft and giving, he was…not.

Then his head ducked close to hers, but his lips merely grazed the point of her chin and followed the line of her jaw toward her ear. "Having me is the easy part."

She shivered and it had nothing to do with the night air. Her fingers latched onto the butter-soft leather jacket covering his wide shoulders.

"But first," he said as he lifted his head with a devilish grin in place, "some celebrating is still in order."

She would have swayed again if not for his steadying hold. "Celebrating?"

"Cake and candles at the very least." He let go of her and in one smooth motion pulled off his jacket and slid it around her shoulders.

The leather hung heavily around her and smelled of him. She managed not to slide into a puddle at his feet and clutched the front of the coat together with one hand. He took the other and pulled her steadily through the dimly lit parking lot, stopping only when they reached the passenger side of a big, dark pickup truck. "If we find a cake at this hour, I'll eat my hat," she told him, trying to curtail the excitement racing through her.

"There are better things to eat." He pulled open the door, ran his hands beneath the jacket to unerringly find her waist, and lifted her right off her feet, sliding her up his long body. "I haven't been tempted to make love to a woman in a parking lot since I was fifteen."

She swallowed hard, shocked by the rush of temptation that centered hot and moist inside her. "I don't…um…do this sort of thing."

"Celebrate your birthday?" His words whispered along her neck.

Her head fell back. "Invite a man to my room. I was planning to get one at the motel across the street."

Whether that was margarita-inspired boldness or Axelinspired boldness, she didn't know, and wasn't sure she cared. They were adults.

"Good," he said, sliding his lips over hers in a faint, grazing kiss that made her pulse throb. "We'll have someplace to go to have our cake—" he slid her slowly onto the seat and tucked her knees inside "—and eat it, too."

Her heart lurched as he closed the door. She watched him through the windows as he rounded the front of the truck. His gaze seemed to meet hers through the window for a moment that started to stretch forever. Then he opened the door and climbed behind the wheel. "Ready?"

"Mmm hmm." It sounded strangled even to her.

He put the keys in the ignition and in seconds they were driving out of the parking lot.

Dear Lord, what had she gotten herself into?

But then he glanced at her and his smile was slow. Oh-so-easy. He gently squeezed her fingers where they were clenched against the side of her seat.

And just that easily, calmness spread through her. Her worries settled. Her judgments dissolved. At that moment, she knew she was exactly where she wanted to be.

With him.

## *Chapter One*

The hearts were everywhere. If anyone entering the high school gymnasium wondered what was being celebrated, the hearts would definitely have given it away.

"How much for these earrings?"

Tara smiled at the pretty teenager standing at her Valentine's Festival booth. It was only February 13th, but the event planners had figured they'd have a better turnout from the residents of Weaver on a Saturday than they would on a Sunday. "They're half off if you turn in a can of food for the food drive." The rest of Tara's profit would go directly to the primary purpose of the festival—raising funds for the elementary school expansion.

The girl handed her the distinctive bead earrings. "Promise you won't sell 'em, okay? I'll be right back."

"I promise." Tara watched the girl speed off across the gymnasium floor that was crowded with booths offering everything from kisses to cookies.

All of the businesses in Weaver had turned out to offer something of interest at the festival. Even Tara. Though the last thing she felt like celebrating was the hearts-and-love thing.

She sat down on the little round stool behind the stylishly draped table that constituted her contribution to the Valentine's Festival. Two more hours and she could pack up shop and move her wares back to Classic Charms, satisfied in the knowledge that she'd done her part in this latest exercise of community spirit.

There was no reason for her to stay after that. The festivities would culminate in the evening's dinner dance and purchasing the ticket didn't mean she had to attend.

The only thing she wanted to do that evening was have an early rendezvous with her four-poster bed. Alone.

"Afternoon, Tara." Hope Clay—one of the festival organizers and the head of the school board—stopped in front of her booth, her violet eyes sparkling behind the stylish glasses she wore. "Looks like business has been good." She touched the jewelry rack that was very nearly empty. "This is the first chance I've had to come by. I was hoping to pick up something for my nieces."

Tara kept her practiced smile in place. She'd already seen more than one of Hope's nieces. "Leandra was by with Lucas on her hip as soon as the doors opened."

Hope laughed, looking younger than the fifty Tara knew her to be, because half the town had been invited to celebrate the milestone. "That little boy may be only two, but he has plenty of Clay blood running in his veins. Tristan and I sat for him and Hannah a few weeks ago. I was exhausted by the time Leandra and Evan picked them up." She shook her head, still grinning. "Not that Lucas is different than any of the other babies in our family."

Hope's gaze caught on a bracelet and she leaned closer to the glass-topped display. "Oh, that one's lovely. Is it amethyst?"

Tara drew out the woven strands of the bracelet and handed it to Hope. "Yes. In fact, Sarah—" yet another one of Hope Clay's nieces "—bought one for Megan about an hour ago. In peridot, though."

Hope glanced at the small price tag hanging from the white-gold clasp. "I wonder what it says when an old lady like me has the same taste as a twelve-year-old girl?"

"Hardly old." Tara's protest was sincere. "And considering the bracelets are my own design," she said as she smiled wryly, "I'd like to think that it says you both have excellent taste."

"Very well said." Hope's husband, Tristan, stopped behind his wife, closing his hand around her nape in a simple gesture that managed to eloquently display years of devotion.

Hope smiled up at her tall husband. "I thought you were going to be tied up with meetings all afternoon. Everything go all right?"

"Unexpectedly so." The man finally slid his attention from his wife's face toward Tara. His brilliant blue gaze crinkled with a timeless appeal. "So, Tara, how much is my wife's excellent taste going to cost me this time?"

Tara told him and he slid the cash out of his wallet. He waved off the receipt she began to write out. Not that she was surprised considering his video-gaming company, CeeVid, had already funded the brunt of the school expansion. The Clays in general were a generous lot when it came to supporting their community.

And then there were *some* Clays who were more like a hit and run.

She pushed aside the thought and finished wrapping up the bracelet in her traditional Classic Charms ivory and silver striped packaging before passing it over to Hope. "There you go. I hope you'll enjoy it."

"Here's my can a' food." The teenager was back, looking

breathless as she handed over an enormous can and a wad of cash. "You didn't sell the earrings, did you?"

Tara pulled them out and handed them to the girl. "I promised I wouldn't."

"I knew this festival would be a good idea," Hope said as she took the can of peaches and set it in the nearly full bin beside Tara's booth. "We'll see you later at the dance. I now have the perfect bracelet to wear with my dress." Waving the pretty box, she moved off on her husband's arm.

Biting back the pinch of envy she felt watching the couple, Tara focused on her young customer. She picked up the wad of cash and began unfolding it. "These earrings are for pierced ears, you know."

"I know. I got my ears pierced last month." The girl held up the dangling earrings that she'd chosen, eyeing them with fervent delight. "These are going to be my first *real* pair when I can take out the studs. Finally." She rolled her eyes. "I thought my dad was never gonna let me pierce my ears."

Tara could identify. Despite his frequent absences, her father had still managed to implacably rule his roost with an iron fist. "Dads can be like that." She gave the girl her change, deftly wrapped the earrings in tissue and popped them into a small box. "There you go."

"Thanks." Holding the box like a treasure, the girl turned on her heel and fairly floated across the gymnasium floor. She didn't even stop at any of the other booths.

Tara sat back down on her stool, glancing at her watch. An hour longer, she told herself, and she could reasonably begin packing up.

Unfortunately, the hour seemed to drag by as customer traffic began to slow.

Her water bottle was long empty, her bladder was long full, and the only thing of interest to watch was the line of eager customers at Courtney Clay's Kissing Booth sitting smack-dab in the center of the gymnasium. Considering the young nurse was strikingly beautiful—and eligible—the line wasn't that surprising.

After a while, Tara turned away, hiding a yawn behind her palm, and reached beneath her table for one of the boxes she'd used to bring in her load that morning. Not quite an hour had passed, but it was close enough for her.

She set the box on her stool and began taking down the unsold garments hanging on the display rack. Slipping them off their hangers, she folded them neatly between tissue paper before placing them in the box. The more careful she was, the less steaming she'd have to do when she hung the clothing back up in her shop.

She filled the first box and put it on the floor, then bent below the table again to hunt down the next box.

"Did you bury a bone down there?" The voice was low. Husky. Amused.

Painfully familiar.

Her heart nearly jumped out of her chest as she warily peered above the table.

She would have welcomed a nonstop procession of Clays, if *this* one would just disappear.

It was, after all, what he was good at.

Looking away from Axel, she dragged another box out.

*Don't look at the guy. That's what got you into trouble last time.*

Trouble.

It was almost laughable, if it weren't so clichéd.

"What are you doing here?" She didn't sound welcoming and wished she didn't care. She would have far preferred to sound breezily unconcerned about his unexpected presence.

"We need to talk."

"After four months of silence? I don't think so." *Darnit. That didn't sound breezy, either.* She grabbed the rest of the hangers from the rack, clothing and all, and shoved the bundle into the box.

If she had to steam out wrinkles until the cows came home, she suddenly didn't care. She just wanted to get out of there. She slapped the lid onto the box and dropped it atop the first.

"Tara—"

But she'd already crouched down to fish out another box. Beneath the cover of the table, she exhaled shakily.

He's just a guy, she told herself for about the millionth time since that night in Braden that had turned into an entire weekend. More than forty-eight hours spent with each other in that little motel room, during which time she'd stupidly started thinking things she'd had no business thinking. Crazy things. Forever things.

All of which had come to a screeching halt when he'd been gone from their bed before she'd woken up that last morning.

The only thing he'd left behind was a note that he'd "call." He'd scrawled the message on the flattened pink bakery box that had held the small chocolate cake he'd managed to track down after searching three different stores.

The cake that—after she'd made a wish and blown out the candles, all of which he'd insisted upon—they'd managed to share over those two days in shockingly creative ways that still haunted her dreams.

But call?

Right.

Not only had he been gone from her bed, but he hadn't shown his face in Weaver afterward. Not the next day. Not the next week. Not the next month.

The thoughts they'd shared. The laughter they'd had. The love they'd made. None of it mattered.

One weekend was all they had in common.

Well, she was a big girl. She would live with the consequences.

She grabbed the storage box and drew it out, squaring her shoulders and straightening her spine in the same motion.

Axel, unfortunately, was still leaning atop the display case, his shoulders seemingly wider than ever beneath the nubby, gray turtleneck sweater he wore.

The last time she'd seen those shoulders, they'd been bare and golden and glistening with sweat while he'd made love to her as if he'd never wanted to stop.

She banished the painfully vivid thought and looked pointedly at the case. "Do you mind?"

He backed away slightly. Ignoring his solid chest only inches away, she flipped open the case and drew out one of the sliding trays from beneath.

"I can explain the four months." His voice was quiet beneath the laughter coming from the nearby kissing booth.

"No explanation needed," she assured him. "It was what it was." There. *That* was breezy. She even managed to top it off with a careless shrug and a small smile. "When did you get back into town?"

"This morning. I intended to call."

Too little, too late. Four months too late.

"No big deal," she said, still breezy.

She was an adult. They'd had a "one-night stand" that happened to last an entire weekend, and the aftereffects were her business and hers alone.

The only thing that bothered her now was that she *was* bothered by his four months' worth of silence.

*Liar. Tell him.*

She ignored the insistent whisper inside her head and with no regard for her usual order, dumped the contents of the jewelry tray into the box. She'd sort it out when she got back to the shop.

"Something important came up," he said. She made the mistake of glancing at him and caught the grimace that crossed his unreasonably handsome face. "I know how that sounds."

"It doesn't matter how it sounds. It was months ago. No big deal. I hardly—" she said as her tongue nearly tripped "—hardly remember much about it."

The corners of his lips lifted ever so slightly. "D'you know that there are five little freckles on your nose that only show up when you lie?"

She shoved the empty tray back in its slot and grabbed the second one. "You've offered the obligatory explanation, but as you can see, I'm busy."

"I don't think I explained anything."

He hadn't, and they both knew it.

What she didn't understand, though, was why he bothered pressing the matter. "Let's just save our breath and say that you did." They'd spent a weekend together and she'd come close to losing her heart. He, on the other hand, had just taken a powder when he'd decided it was time to go.

He grabbed the tray before she could shake its contents into the box. "Tara."

She wasn't going to engage in a tug-of-war over a jewelry tray. Nor was she going to get into any sort of conversation about what had occurred between them when there were still too many people around who could overhear.

Gossip was going to be rife enough about her soon without anyone overhearing *that*.

She let go of the tray and reached for the last one, pulling it out and tipping it into the box.

He muttered an oath and set down the tray. "Tara—"

"Axel Clay, is that you?" A bright, female voice accosted them from across the gymnasium.

"We *will* talk," he told Tara before turning to greet the curly-haired blonde aiming for him. "Hey, Dee. How's it going?"

The young woman unabashedly threw her arms around him, giving him an exuberant hug. "I'm going to have to give Sarah a lashing. She didn't tell me you were coming home.

We all thought you were still in Europe trying to buy up some fancy horse. Hi, Tara," she added absently.

Under other circumstances, Tara would probably have been amused by Deirdre Crowder's actions. Dee was a teacher at the elementary school. She and Sarah Scalise—another teacher *and* Axel's cousin—were frequent visitors to Classic Charms.

But it wasn't "other circumstances," and the day had taken its toll on Tara's humor.

She was fresh out.

She nevertheless managed a casual response for Dee and took advantage of Axel's diverted attention to quickly finish unloading the jewelry case. She couldn't help but overhear Axel telling Dee that his cousin hadn't known about his arrival. She also couldn't help but notice the way Dee kept her slender fingers latched onto Axel's arm.

"Excuse me," she told Dee, whose other hand was near the display case.

"Sorry." Dee moved her hand, but didn't take her attention away from Axel. "So, how long are you going to be around? We ought to all get together."

Tara hefted the acrylic display unit off the table and perched it on the boxes, then slid out from behind the booth. She still needed to disassemble the clothing rack but she wasn't going to listen to Dee, avowed man-hunter that she was, set up a date with Axel.

Without looking at them, she made her way to the storage room to retrieve her handcart that she'd left there after unloading her wares earlier that day. She pulled it out, struggling with the recalcitrant folding mechanism.

"Let me help you with that."

Her shoulders drooped. Dee hadn't kept Axel's attention nearly long enough to suit her. That fact was probably as displeasing to Dee as it was to Tara.

"I don't need help." She jerked on the cart handles and it sprang into place. Her fingers narrowly avoided being pinched, but she gave Axel a smooth smile. "See?"

She wheeled the cart smartly around his tall form and headed back toward her booth. Her legs were no match for his, though, and he beat her there, only to block the boxes as if it would take dynamite to dislodge him.

Her lips tightened and she turned to the clothing rack, deftly dismantling the rods to fit into the last box. Still ignoring him, she pulled on her coat—a new one since she'd lost hers completely that night at the Suds-n-Grill—and wrapped her scarf around her neck. Pulling the loaded cart, she headed toward the gymnasium exit.

She hadn't reached it yet when Joe Gage, the tall, balding elementary school principal, stepped through it. "Shutting down shop, Tara?" He held the glass door wide for her.

"I am. Thanks, Joe." She maneuvered the cart through the doorway.

"We'll see you at the dance tonight, right? This old guy expects to share a dance with you." He grinned, a perfectly appealing man who'd been nothing but friendly to Tara in all the time she'd lived there.

She smiled and hoped he didn't realize she hadn't answered.

Behind Joe's shoulder she could see Axel, purpose in his stride.

"Hey, Ax," she heard Joe greet him as she hurried along the sidewalk. "Didn't know you were back in town."

She walked faster, not listening for Axel's response. Her breath was hitching in her chest when she finally made it to her white SUV.

She set the cart upright and fished her keys out of her pocket to unlock the rear gate. It hadn't even completely swung open when Axel arrived.

Her lips tightened but she stepped out of the way when he

plucked the top box off the stack and slid it into the rear of her vehicle. He followed it up with the rest of her boxes, then with annoying ease, folded up the cart, turned it sideways, and slid it alongside the boxes.

He slammed the gate shut and turned his penetrating eyes her way. His sharply angled jaw was set. "You can either talk to me now, or talk to me later. But we will talk, Tara. There are things you need to know."

And one gigantic thing she wasn't ready for him—or anyone else in town, for that matter—to know.

But her time on that score was rapidly diminishing.

Not for the first time, she wondered why she didn't just leave Weaver altogether. Her shop was a modest success there, but that was the only thing keeping her in the small town. That and the fact that it was the only place her brother knew where to reach her.

She bunched the key chain inside her fist. "I want to get these things returned to the store before the dance tonight."

"Then I'll come with you."

"No!" The word came out more sharply than she intended, particularly when she could see people just a few rows away. "I—I'll be at the dance," she lied as she headed to the driver's side door.

"That's not the best place."

It was the perfect place since she had no intention of being there.

She yanked open the door and climbed inside. "Take it or leave it," she said and shut the door between them.

Then she pretended that her hands weren't shaking as she shoved the key in the ignition and drove away like the bats of hell were hard on her heels.

Only Axel Clay was no bat.

He was the only man she'd slept with since her marriage of a minute when she'd been eighteen.

He was the man who'd left her flat after a weekend she couldn't seem to get out of her heart or her head.

But worst of all, he was the father of the baby she was carrying.

## *Chapter Two*

Axel stifled an oath as he watched the white SUV roar out of the school parking lot. He looked up at the pale winter sky and blew out a breath that made rings around his head.

No matter what Tara had said, he doubted that she'd be back for the dance that evening. What had he expected? That she'd welcome him back with open arms?

He'd had plenty of female encounters in his life; all with women who had played by exactly the same rules as he had. That weekend in Braden with Tara, though, had been different. *She* was different. She always had been. Right from the first time he'd met her, five years earlier.

His pocket buzzed slightly, and he pulled out his vibrating cell phone, flipping it open. "Axel here."

"Have you talked to her?" His uncle's voice greeted him.

Axel stared after her but the SUV was already out of sight. "Not exactly."

"This situation isn't open for *inexactly.* Sloan McCray is

a valuable contact for us and I've given him my word that we'll continue taking care of his sister. I want daily reports."

Tristan Clay wasn't only Axel's uncle. He was his boss and he'd made his points plain already. Not that Axel could blame him after the mess he'd made of his last assignment for Hollins-Winword.

The primary concern of the highly secretive agency was security, whether on a personal scale or an international one. At times, they even worked—to use the term loosely—along with governmental agencies, handling matters that couldn't be handled through normal channels. Such was Axel's last assignment, which had been a monumental failure.

He hadn't kept anyone safe, particularly Sloan McCray's lover.

As a result, Tristan had done exactly what he should have done. He'd put Axel on suspension. Which was where Axel had remained until earlier that day when he'd met with his uncle, fully intending to tender the resignation from Hollins-Winword that he'd been holding off on ever since he'd earned that suspension.

Ironically, Axel hadn't resigned.

Instead, he'd found himself nearly begging his uncle for this latest assignment. Not because of his record with Sloan McCray. But because of the assignment, herself.

Tara Browning.

The fact that she was McCray's sister only made the situation that much more complicated for Axel.

Considering everything, it was a wonder that Tristan had agreed. After all, Sloan must have discovered that Tristan had sent Axel to the Suds-n-Grill that night four months ago and kept right on moving, despite the fact that he'd arranged to meet his sister there, too. But Tristan had agreed to give Axel the assignment and though McCray had pitched a mighty fit about it, he wasn't in a position to demand someone else.

"Daily reports," Axel assured him, disconnecting before Tristan could decide to change his mind.

He strode through the crowded parking lot until he reached his truck, parked blatantly in a No Parking zone.

The parking ticket tucked beneath his windshield wiper waved gaily in the biting breeze.

He yanked the paper out and climbed in the truck. He shoved the ticket into the glove box where it joined a couple dozen others, a tire gauge and his holstered GLOCK.

He'd barely gotten his key in the ignition when the phone buzzed again. "Yeah?"

"Is that how you *always* answer your phone?"

He grimaced at his mother's familiar voice and started up the truck. "I guess you've heard." There was nothing like the Weaver grapevine when it came to spreading news, whether you wanted it spread or not.

"That you're back in town?" Emily Clay's voice was tart, but beneath it he could still hear the love that had always been a constant. "Imagine my pleasure hearing it from someone other than you. I've gotten three different calls from people reporting that they've seen your truck driving down Main Street."

"Sorry. I had some business to take care of."

"With Evan, I imagine," Emily concluded, making Axel feel that much guiltier.

"I haven't talked to Evan, yet," he admitted, knowing perfectly well that she was probably already aware of that fact. Evan Taggart was the local vet and his brother-in-law, but they'd thrown in together to breed horses even before Evan had married Axel's sister, Leandra.

The business partnership was real and increasingly profitable. It also provided a highly convenient cover for Axel's other activities. Activities of which Evan had always been aware, even before Axel's own immediate family had been.

"Hmm," Emily was saying. "And when will you be making your way out to the farm?"

The "farm" was Clay Farm, the larger and considerably more significant horse farm owned by his parents outside of town. It was where he'd grown up and where he always returned. Never before, however, had he returned with the weight on his conscience that he had now, and there was no denying his reluctance.

It was the same reluctance that had dogged him when it came to returning to Weaver at all.

"Soon," he said. "I still have things to take care of in town."

"There's a Valentine's dance at the high school tonight. Your father and I will be there."

"I stopped at the gym already. Looked in."

"Did you see Courtney, then? She's doing the kissing booth this year, if you can believe it."

The last time he'd seen his cousin Courtney, she'd been inconsolable at the memorial service that her parents, Rebecca and Sawyer, had finally held for their missing son, Ryan.

"She had a line stretching around the gym," Axel said. "I didn't want to get in the way of the moneymaking."

"It's just good to see her having some fun again. Since Ryan's service last year, she's had a tough time."

There was nothing Axel could say to that. Not now. He couldn't exactly tell his mother the real reason he'd avoided Ryan's little sister, now could he?

Ryan had made him promise.

"Did you run into Hope or Tristan?" his mother continued.

"Not at the festival." At least that was the truth. He'd met with Tristan at his office over at CeeVid.

"Then if you're still in town, come by the dance."

If he believed that Tara had any intention of going to the dance, he'd be there all right. As it was, from here on out, he was going to be where Tara was. "We'll see."

His mother just "hmmed" again as if reading his mind. She'd always known when he was up to something.

"You do realize that tomorrow is Sunday, right?" Emily said after a moment. "If I don't see you tonight, I'm certainly going to expect to see you tomorrow."

Axel pinched the bridge of his nose. "Who's got Sunday dinner this week?" His mom and his aunts all rotated the duty. Sometimes it was just a handful of family members who were there. Sometimes it was the entire freaking family.

All two hundred of them.

It was an exaggeration, but sometimes it felt as if it were only a slight one.

"Jaimie's cooking," his mother answered. "We'll be at the big house."

At the Double-C Ranch then, where his father and uncles had been raised and where his grandfather, Squire, and his wife Gloria, still lived with Axel's aunt and uncle—Matthew and Jaimie. Going there felt no less of a betrayal, though, than it did going to his own home. "Is everyone going to be there?"

"It's been over a year since you've been home, honey. What do you think?"

*Way* too many family members is what he thought. "If you don't see me until tomorrow afternoon, don't worry."

"I always worry about you. It's what mothers do."

He caught a glimpse of himself in the rearview mirror after they hung up, and he looked away. He didn't want to think about mothers and sons just now.

Which spoke directly to the reason why he'd been reluctant to come back to Weaver at all. He had a good family. To the last one, they were *all* good.

None of them deserved the secret he was keeping from them about Ryan.

But if he didn't keep Ryan's secret, Axel was more afraid

that his cousin would go even deeper underground and it had taken Axel too long to find him in the first place.

Maybe he couldn't do anything about his own family. But he could definitely do something about McCray's family.

He pulled away from the curb and headed back toward Main Street where Classic Charms was located. He trolled past, drumming his thumb on the steering wheel as he studied the light he could see burning inside her eclectic little shop.

He could either sit in the warmth of his truck and watch the shop, or he could brave the frost—both from the weather and from her—and go talk with her.

Make her understand the gravity of the situation.

It would have been a helluva lot easier to do that if he hadn't already done the unforgivable by getting involved with her that weekend in Braden.

He'd been ordered to that bar by Tristan for a quick "meet" with McCray. The last person Axel had expected to see there was the man's sister.

But there she'd been.

From his corner in the bar, he'd watched her sit by herself for more than an hour. Watched the way her gleaming, dark hair would slip from behind her ear where she kept tucking it. Watched her debate with herself each time the cocktail waitress came by to replenish her drink. Watched the way half the men in the place watched her, and the way she'd seemed oblivious to them all.

Most particularly, he'd watched the fading of animation from her lovely face the longer she sat there alone, leaving her enormous brown eyes looking darker and more haunting than ever.

He shouldn't have stepped in her way when she was leaving. But he had.

And damned if he could make himself regret it even if

Tristan could now yank him from his assignment to protect her if he found out about that night.

She was a petite package of feminine curves who didn't even reach his shoulder. He'd been halfway beyond crazy over her from the first time he'd seen her when she'd moved to Weaver, five years earlier.

The fact that she'd been placed there for her own safety by none other than his uncle Tristan had kept Axel from acting on his feelings.

That night in Braden, though, his attraction had been more alive than ever. And he'd been on the verge of giving Tristan his resignation.

He blew out a rough breath along with the justifications that amounted to zero. He shouldn't have touched her and he knew it. No matter how unforgettable their time had been.

He pulled a U-turn and parked in front of her shop. Her front door was a fanciful thing of stained glass. It was locked, of course. He knocked purposefully as he looked through the glass window beside the door.

He couldn't see her moving around inside, but that wasn't surprising. The place was artfully packed with furniture, clothing and a host of other doodads.

He knocked again, as hard as he dared against a deep red triangle of glass.

Finally, she appeared.

The sleeves of her thigh-length pink sweater were pushed up above her elbows. She'd twisted her hair up into some kind of knot that wasn't particularly effective, judging by the strands of hair that had slipped free to graze her elfin chin.

She made a face when she reached the door and tapped the sign that she'd posted in the lower corner of the window.

Closed.

"I'm not going away, Tara." He knew she could hear him through the glass.

"Leave me alone. Or do I have to call the sheriff?"

"Call him," he said easily. "I haven't seen Max in a year. Good chance to catch up."

"Must be nice to count half the people in town as a relation."

Sometimes it was as much a curse as a blessing. "Open up."

Her bow-shaped lips tightened and she made no move to unlock the door. "Can't you take no for an answer?"

"No." A gust of wind blew down the street, bringing with it a rolling cloud of old snow. "So you might as well let me in."

She looked past him to the street. Whether it was his truck parked there or the sedan slowly driving past that made her grimace he couldn't tell. Didn't much care, considering she finally reached over and with a rattle of keys, opened the door.

"You could have at least parked in the alley behind the building," she muttered, as she shut and locked the door again once he stepped inside. "Everyone in town can recognize your truck."

Warmth engulfed him. "So?"

"So, I don't want people wondering why you're hanging around me."

On that score, she was going to be sadly disappointed.

"Don't bother taking that off," she warned when he unzipped his jacket. "You won't be staying long."

He slid out of the jacket anyway and dropped it on the U-shaped mahogany bar that served as a counter in the center of the store. "There's been a hit issued against your brother," he said bluntly.

For a long moment, her wide eyes just stared at him. Then she slowly blinked. "Excuse me?"

"You heard me. There's a price on Sloan's head."

The lovely throat that he knew tasted as sweet as cream worked in a hard swallow. She abruptly sat down on a weathered-looking leather couch whose massive lines made her look even more defenseless. "H-how would you know that?"

"Because I work for the same agency that placed you in Weaver when your brother went undercover with the ATF."

Her face blanched and he quickly moved to her, placing his hand against her back. "Put your head down."

But she pushed him away. "You *know* Sloan? Is—" she swallowed visibly "—is he all right? He's still under protection somewhere in Chicago, right?"

Truthfully, Axel wasn't entirely certain where Sloan was. The man had shunned the normal protocols and who could blame him? "He's keeping contact," he said instead, truthfully enough, though Tristan was the only one with whom McCray was maintaining the briefest of communications.

He eyed Tara's fearful expression and shoved his hands in his pockets to keep from reaching for her again.

There had already been too much touching between them. He was still losing sleep from the burning memory of those white-hot hours they'd shared. "How much do you know about the case he's been working on?"

She swiped a strand of hair from her cheek. "Only that when he infiltrated the Deuce's Cross, he wanted me far away from Chicago just in case the gang suspected he wasn't the ex-con he was pretending to be." Her hands fell back to her lap. "He was exaggerating the situation. Nothing's ever happened to me. Not during the years he rode with them, and certainly not in the time it's taken to get the case to trial." She looked around the shop, avoiding eye contact. "I gave up the only home I've ever known to come here. It's temporary. Just until all that's over."

Five years didn't seem all that temporary to Axel, but he kept the thought to himself. "A few years before Sloan was finally accepted into the gang, another federal agent had gotten in. But his cover was blown. They killed his family before they executed him." There was nothing he could do to soften the facts. They were what they were.

And they were only part of the reason behind Sloan's rightful concern, now.

But Axel still felt like a bastard when her face paled all over again. His hands fisted in his pockets. It was either that, or reach for her, and he was pretty certain she'd push him away. Again.

"The Feds couldn't make a murder case stick at that point," he continued quietly. "Your brother was the one who finally came up with the glue." About murder and a host of other felonies. "Now that the trial is finally going forward, it's likely they want payback more than ever."

"But Sloan's identity was supposed to be protected."

"There's no guarantee about that," he said carefully. "Information has a way of getting out. Your brother's not taking any chances that it might lead to you."

"I don't even use my maiden name. I've spoken with Sloan once in the past five years! I don't have a phone number for him or even an address. All I can do is sit around on my thumbs waiting for him to contact me." She grimaced. "And to blow me off again even after he has. Why...*why* would anything about my brother lead to me?"

"You're not some far-flung relation of his. You're his twin sister." Sloan's only living family.

Her lips compressed. "So what am I supposed to do? Give up everything again and go start somewhere new?"

He frowned at the assessment. "Right now, Weaver is still the best place for you."

"And how long have you known about all of this?"

"You mean about the order on Sloan, or the reason you moved to Weaver?"

She looked ill. "Both."

He finally pulled his hands out of his pockets. "Since this morning, and since you came to town five years ago."

"Great." Her expression grew even more pinched. "So all

that talk in Braden about your horse-breeding business was just a story. A line. You're with the ATF, too."

They hadn't just talked about his business. They'd talked about hers. About movies and books and politics and religion. And they'd made love. Again. And again.

"I didn't lie to you. I *am* a horse breeder."

"But that's not all you are," she said her voice flat. "Right?"

"No," he allowed. "But I'm not with the ATF."

"But you said you were with the agency—"

"The ATF didn't move you here to Wyoming. An agency called Hollins-Winword did that."

Her lips parted. "But Sloan told me—"

He lifted his hand. "It doesn't matter." In a perfect world, the ATF would have been able to see to the full protection of its own agents. But he'd learned long ago that the world wasn't perfect. McCray had done what Axel would have done in the same situation. He'd found someone to take care of what his own agency wouldn't. "Sloan trusted Hollins-Winword to keep you safe before, and Hollins-Winword is going to keep you safe now."

She closed her eyes for a moment as if she were searching for strength. He started to reach for her no matter the chances of rejection but she planted her slender palms on her knees and pushed abruptly to her feet.

Her brown eyes looked like bruises against her pale face. "Fine. You've told me. *Now* will you go?" She started toward the door. "Your five minutes are long gone."

He closed his hand around her arm and absorbed the frisson that raced through him at the contact. "It's more than a matter of just keeping you updated on the situation."

She'd gone still the moment he touched her. Her gaze seemed focused on his hand on her arm. "Meaning what?"

"Meaning, I'm your new bodyguard."

## *Chapter Three*

Tara wasn't certain she'd heard right. "Bodyguard."

But Axel didn't correct her. He just stood there, watching her with that steady, golden-brown gaze that she couldn't get out of her mind, while his hand seemed to burn like some branding iron through her long sleeve.

She shook off the ridiculous notion. She wasn't branded by this man any more than she was going to put up with this bodyguard nonsense.

"No." Her voice was flat and she headed straight for the door. "No. No. And *no*."

"It isn't your choice."

She pulled open the door. "It most certainly is. Just like it's my choice to tell you to leave." For years, she'd lived a life that she hadn't chosen for herself, all for the benefit of Sloan's overprotective streak. She'd gone along with it then because he'd asked her to, and there wasn't anything she wouldn't have done for him.

He was not just family—her *only* family—he'd been her best friend. She was his "goober" and he was her "bean."

Now her brother was more of a stranger who seemed to be glad she was out of his hair.

As for Axel—it was best that he get out of *her* hair. "I want you to leave. Now."

He surprised her by actually moving toward the door. But he stopped before passing through, standing so closely that she could feel the warmth of him. His head tilted toward her and it was all she could do to keep from trembling. "One way or another I will be guarding you, Tara. You'll make it a lot easier if you work with me on it."

So much for not trembling.

She hoped he'd attribute it to the cold air curling around them and not the effect he had on her. "I don't feel compelled to make your life easier." She wanted there to be plenty of distance between them before it became evident to anyone who looked at her that she wasn't looking quite as thin as she ordinarily did.

Unexpected pregnancies weren't just the domain of the young and foolish. She was a competent adult, and she'd still gotten "caught." For now, though, nobody but her obstetrician in Braden knew.

"Darlin'," he said, his voice dropping another notch, "there isn't anything *easy* about this," he assured her and stepped out onto the sidewalk outside her door.

She firmly shut it, staring at him through the mottled stained glass as she deliberately set the locks.

"I'm not going to let this drop," he warned.

"Then you'll be wasting a lot of time," she answered, and hated the tightness in her throat. She made herself turn away from the door. Ignoring all of the items that needed to be returned to the shelves, she headed straight to the rear door, barely stopping long enough to hit the light switches and grab her coat.

She got in her car that was parked out back and, half-afraid she'd see his big truck rolling into view, bolted down the alley with a shameless disregard for caution. Less then ten minutes later, she'd pulled into the garage beside her house.

Axel hadn't followed her.

She told herself she wasn't surprised.

His "bodyguard" threat was just that. A threat.

Which didn't explain at all why, once inside, she kept peering through the plantation shutters at the windows for any sight of his truck.

When she realized the street lights had come on outside, she wanted to tear out her hair. She'd wasted at least an hour padding from window to window. Watching and waiting for Axel to appear. Or worse.

Stomping to her closet, she gave a practiced yank on the enameled doorknob, hard enough to spring the stubborn, warped door open. She snatched out the first decent dress her hand encountered. She tossed it on the bed, then went down the hall to the bathroom.

Her reflection in the ancient mirror showed flushed cheeks and too-dark eyes. She freed her hair from the clip, pulling a brush through it until it swung smooth again, and swabbed some cosmetics into place. Then she went back into the bedroom where she put on the knee-length dress.

It was black, which suited her mood, with a forgivingly swinging cut that didn't cling anywhere except where the wide, scooped neckline hugged the points of her shoulders. She pulled on black nylons—managing to put a run in the first pair she tried—shoved her feet into shiny black pumps, added a jet-black choker and drop earrings that she'd made a few years ago, and headed to the door.

The Valentine's dance was the last place she wanted to be, but it was still better than hovering around in the shadows of her house, watching for signs of Axel Clay.

Her coat was where she'd left it by the back door and she slipped into it before leaving the house to cross the cracked sidewalk leading to the garage.

She resolutely ignored the way her neck prickled before she reached the safety of her car and drove it out onto the street, heading back to the school.

When she arrived, the gymnasium had once again been transformed. This time into a dinner dance, complete with a live band playing with more enthusiasm than skill on the stage that had been erected at one end. Large round tables were situated along the sides of the room—most of which already looked full. Opposite the stage, several long tables had been set up as a buffet, where there was already a long line.

And of course there were the hearts. Everywhere.

She blew out a faint breath as she handed over her ticket to the teenagers manning the entry and slid out of her coat, leaving it in the area set aside for them.

There was no such thing as a coat check in Weaver, Wyoming.

The fact that her car keys were in the coat pocket niggled at her, which annoyed her to no end. If it weren't for Axel Clay's ridiculous claim, she wouldn't have thought twice about them.

"Good evening, Tara." Joe Gage greeted her within seconds after she'd passed over her ticket. "You look great." His gaze ran down her with appreciation. Sadly, she felt none of the rippling aftereffects from *his* attention that she did from Axel. She didn't look at Joe and then have foolish, romantic thoughts of happily-ever-afters twining around her better sense.

"Thanks. So do you." The school principal did look nice, but he certainly didn't make her mouth water. Now that she was pregnant, this was certainly no time to start encouraging him, but desperate times called for desperate measures. "Looks like quite a crowd here tonight." She was probably the only one in town who'd bought a ticket with no intention of using it.

"Yeah." His gaze was diverted by Dee Crowder who sailed past them looking pretty in a lacy red dress. "There's a seat left at my table, though."

"Thanks—" The word caught when she felt a warm, long-fingered hand slide over her shoulder from behind.

"Thanks, Joe," Axel said from above her head, "but we should probably find a spot for two." His chuckle was deep. "Not that I'd mind Tara sitting on my lap through dinner."

She stared up at him. "What do—"

His hand squeezed her shoulder. Not hard. But definitely in warning.

The rest of her protest died in her throat.

Her cheeks warmed at the realization crossing Joe's face when he took in Axel's proprietary hand, and she felt even worse when Joe smiled despite the disappointment in his eyes. "I wouldn't mind if the prettiest woman in the room had to sit on my lap for a while, either." He looked back over the crowded tables. "Most of your family is already here. Back near the buffet tables." He grinned. "Y'all take up more than a few tables."

"Principal Gage." Dee Crowder reappeared. She had a pink cocktail in her hand and curiosity in her face as she eyed Axel's hand on Tara, too. "Mind if I take the last seat at your table?"

"Of course I don't mind. Axel, Tara, enjoy the evening," he told them before tucking his hand in Dee's arm. Tara felt her chance of sitting safely well away from the Clays evaporating as Joe escorted Dee to his table.

"Come on." Axel urged her forward, right into the melee of dancers taking up the narrow rectangle in the center of the gymnasium floor. "Let's dance."

It was a double-edged reprieve from being forced to go to his family's tables. "I don't dance." Déjà vu accosted her as he turned her into his arms.

"Think we've been over that," he murmured, flattening her curled fingers against his shoulder.

The last thing she needed was a reminder of their time in Braden. Particularly when she now had a constant reminder, courtesy of her thickening waistline. And when Axel's hand slid around that waist, she couldn't help but hold her breath, just waiting for him to make some comment.

But though his fingertips seemed to flex against her, all he said was a muttered "Relax."

She felt a hysterical bubble of laughter rise in her. Relax? "You've got to be kidding."

His head lowered until his mouth was near her ear. "Honey, I've never been more serious." He pulled her even closer. Until her breasts were flat against him and their legs were nearly entwined.

She could feel each one of his fingers splayed against her spine. "How do I know this isn't all something you've made up, anyway? I've never heard of this Hollins thing you're talking about."

He smoothly spun her around. "Keep your voice down."

"Nobody can hear me." How could they when he wasn't allowing a centimeter of breathing room between them?

"You never know who might hear what." His lips brushed against her ear again and a shiver danced down her spine that owed nothing to memory and everything to the present. "And someday I might be curious as to why you'd think I'd make up a story like this. But for now, just know that most people never have a reason to learn about the agency. And that's a good thing."

She was perfectly aware that Axel's answer hadn't provided any proof at all to back up his claim. Nor did she feel inclined to tell him that she was used to people making up stories to suit whatever agenda they had in mind. Her father had been the absolute master at it.

She realized her cheek was feeling much too comfortable against his soft sweater. Or maybe it was the incredibly hard chest beneath the gray knit that was too comfortable.

She lifted her head, but that only put her forehead right beneath his angular chin. "Not that I believe any of this, but Sloan is notoriously overprotective." Maybe the trait was a result of their childhood. She had her own issues that had carried over into adulthood, too. That's what happened when you were raised by a man whose career demanded secrecy. "And I can handle my own safety."

Axel's hand crept an inch lower, moving dangerously near the small of her back. "Did I tell you how beautiful you look tonight?"

She deliberately stepped on his foot and wished it were so easy to squash the memory of his lips touching that very same spot where his fingers were drifting. "Sorry."

She caught the twitch of his lips. "You're not. But it's natural that you're in a defensive mode. I've thrown you a curve."

Again, she felt that hysterical bubble want to escape. If he only knew. "How…understanding of you." She tried to wedge her hand between them to create at least a minimum of breathing space.

Instead, he just covered her hand with his, probably looking even more loverlike to anyone watching them. "You're going to give people the wrong idea." Her heart was pounding and she was painfully aware that he was the reason. Not what he was saying. But *him.*

"The wrong idea about what? That I like dancing with you?" His fingertips flexed again. "I do."

"Well, I don't."

She felt his lips against her temple. His thumb stroked against the wrist he still held captive. "Liar. Your pulse feels like it wants to jump out of your skin."

"Anger does that, too."

She didn't hear the sigh he gave, but she definitely felt it.

"I wasn't joking when I said this would be easier with your cooperation. If you want me dogging your footsteps looking like some stalker, then I will."

She wanted to tear herself out of his arms and run far, far away. Instead, she followed his lead as he wove her around the crowded dance floor in time to the endless ballads that the band was cranking out. "I told you. I can take care of myself."

She felt him sigh again. His jaw brushed against her cheek, the healthy five o'clock shadow he'd developed softly abrading. "Want me to tell you how that other agent's family was killed? How they were going through their normal day, never suspecting, never knowing that—"

"Stop." Her stomach rolled suddenly. "I don't want the details."

"And I don't want to give them," he assured her softly. "But I will if that's what it takes to prove I'm serious." He turned her smoothly to avoid colliding with another couple, and his voice dropped even lower. "We don't know for certain that the order on Sloan came down from the Deuces. But it's pretty likely, considering their trial starts next week. If you won't go along with this for yourself, then do it for Sloan. Protecting people is one of the things I do, Tara. So let me do my job." His deep voice was gentle.

Seductive.

And she had to brace herself against all of it.

"Then protect Sloan."

"He's not my assignment. You are."

Assignments. Jobs.

His insistence had everything to do with his job and nothing to do with her, personally.

Nothing to do with the days they'd spent in each other's arms. Certainly nothing to do with the repercussions of those hours. Repercussions of which he was blissfully unaware.

A state of secrecy she wanted to preserve more now, than ever.

A very short, very brief fling was the only thing she shared with this man. But she and her baby were a team now. She'd realized that in the two months since she'd learned she was pregnant.

She'd never be alone again.

No matter how easily she'd fallen for Axel over the course of one weekend four months ago, neither she nor the baby needed a man as unreliable as *her* father had been in their lives.

"Thanks, but no thanks." She finally succeeded in tugging her hands out of his and stepped away when the song finished and Hope Clay took the microphone to encourage everyone to hit the newly replenished buffet.

"If you'll excuse me," she said loudly enough for anyone to overhear, "I have some people I'd like to say hello to." Without waiting for him to voice the protest forming on his perfectly shaped lips, she turned and joined the mass of people moving off the dance floor in the general direction of the food.

But she didn't join the line that was even longer now than it had been, nor did she have anyone with whom she particularly wanted to speak. Instead, she slipped through the door leading to the girl's locker room.

Only there was no easy escape there, either, she realized at the sight of Axel's mother standing at the row of sinks, drying her hands on a paper towel.

"Hello, Tara." Emily Clay's dark hair was swept up with a sparkling clip and—like half the women present—she looked Valentine-appropriate in a slender red cocktail sheath. "What a lovely dress you're wearing."

Feeling painfully self-conscious, Tara swished her hand down her dress. "It's just something I grabbed."

"You grabbed," Emily repeated humorously. "Don't say

that around too many women or you might make more enemies than friends. Not all of us can just whip something out of the closet and look like you do."

Tara didn't need the long mirror that spanned the row of sinks to know that her face was turning red. "I think you're describing yourself more than me, but, um, thank you." She knew she wasn't beautiful. She was short and mostly unremarkable with freckles on her nose that makeup didn't always hide, and now she was wearing a dress designed to hide the fact that she was starting to look fat.

Emily, fortunately, didn't seem to notice anything amiss as she tossed her paper towel in the trash bin and headed for the door. "Be sure and bring my errant son by our tables," she told Tara with a wry smile as she left. "He's obviously focused entirely on you, but I have yet to see his face since he got back to town."

It was nearly impossible to keep her smile in place as her face flamed. She murmured something nonsensical, but it didn't matter, because Emily moved out of the way so the giggling teens who'd manned the ticket table could enter and the door swung closed once more.

Tara returned the girls' greetings and needlessly washed her hands. Then, instead of taking the door that led back to the gymnasium, she let herself out through the opposite side, ending up on the cold expanse of cement leading to the outdoor racquetball courts.

Her breath ringed around her head and the cold night air sent goose bumps along her limbs as she hurried along the cement. She'd walk around the building, go in the front again to retrieve her coat and car keys, and then head back home.

Simple enough.

Until she rounded the last corner and stopped short at the sight of Axel, leaning indolently against the building, her coat draped over his crossed arms.

"Forget something?" He lifted the coat with one hand. Her keys were in his other and he jingled them.

She went over to him and snatched both away, half-afraid that he'd refuse to give them to her. But he did, and she yanked her coat over her shoulders, turning toward the parking lot. "Your mother is looking for you."

He ignored that and followed her. "I'm not going away, Tara."

She wanted to press her hands over her ears. Instead, she quickened her steps until she was practically jogging through the rows of vehicles. Then her foot hit a patch of ice and she gasped, throwing out her hands to stop her fall. But she never made contact with the pavement.

Axel scooped her up from behind. "Easy there." His voice was soft against her neck.

She strained against his arm, but it was immovable. "Let me go." The words were garbled. Just as garbled as her vision thanks to the stupid tears that burned her eyes.

"I'm not going to hurt you." He settled her carefully on her feet and muttered an oath when he saw her tears. "Ah, hell. Don't cry. I can take most anything but you crying."

That did *not* help. She felt the tears spill over her lashes and blamed the hormones pelting around inside her for her deplorable lack of control. "I'm *so* sorry you're uncomfortable!" She swiped her cheeks but it was as effective as sticking her thumb in a leaking dam. "Why won't you just leave me alone?"

He was silent, his expression unreadable. "I can't."

"Why not? Because of this story about Sloan? Nobody would make the mistake of thinking I matter to him, least of all me."

"You're wrong."

"How do *you* know?"

"Because I know him." His voice was soft—as soft as it had been in the middle of the dance floor, but his words still seemed to echo around her.

"Well, I'm glad you do, because I don't. Not anymore." She

tried peeling Axel's fingers away from where they were wrapped around her waist and the bunched lapels of her coat. "And I only have your word about all of this. So—"

He exhaled and released her. "Why on God's green earth would I make any of this up?"

Certainly not because he'd need such a line to get close to her. She'd already proven how easy *that* was.

"I don't know," she admitted and turned again to head for her SUV. She could see it just four vehicles over. "And frankly, I don't care," she said over her shoulder as she walked, more carefully this time, toward it.

She squashed her biting conscience.

After all. What was one more lie between them?

## *Chapter Four*

If he followed her home, Tara wasn't sure what she would do. But she didn't see any sight of Axel's truck in her rearview mirror as she drove straight home from the high school.

That didn't seem to keep her foot from hitting the gas harder than necessary, though.

She parked in the garage and when she realized she'd locked the car door, she exhaled, annoyed, and unlocked it again. This was *Weaver,* for heaven's sake.

Nothing bad ever happened here, no matter what Axel said.

She went inside the house, dumped her coat over the back of a kitchen table chair and filled the teapot with water before setting it on the stove.

Which wouldn't light.

Kicking the old stove would do nothing but scuff her pumps, so she refrained, but it took a deep exhale to stop herself. She lit the pilot light again and tried the burner. The small flame jumped to life beneath the teapot and leaving it to heat, she kicked off her shoes and carried them with her to her bedroom.

The shutters at the windows beckoned, but she resolutely avoided looking out and exchanged her party clothes for her long chenille robe. Back in the kitchen, she dropped an herbal tea bag in a mug and took the shrilly whistling teapot off the stove again.

Only when the whistling dwindled did she hear the doorbell ringing.

Since nobody *ever* came to her door, she didn't have to guess hard who might be on her front porch.

There was no law that said she had to answer the door, she reasoned.

Only to go to the door and yank it open, anyway.

Axel stood there with his finger pressed steadily against the doorbell.

"Leave me alone."

He lowered his finger and stuck a cell phone out at her. "Say hello," he said evenly.

She eyed the phone. "Excuse me?"

He put the phone to his ear. "Your sister will be on in a second," he said.

For a moment, her brain seemed to stop working. But then her senses returned and she glared at Axel. "I don't know what sort of game you're—"

"Seconds are precious here, Tara," he interrupted.

She snatched the phone out of his hand. Held it to her ear. "Hello."

"I'm sorry I couldn't make it on our birthday," her brother's voice greeted her.

She nearly dropped the phone. "Who *is* this?"

"Goober, just do what Clay tells you, and I'll explain things later."

Her eyes closed. *Goober.* Her brother's nickname for her

when they were kids. Who else but he would know that? The McCrays had never stayed put anywhere long enough for other people to take note of them. "Sloan—"

But the connection was already dead.

She still held the phone to her ear, though, as if by some miracle she could reestablish that much-too-brief contact.

Finally, Axel slid the phone out of her numb fingers and pushed her gently inside the door.

She couldn't even muster a protest when he nudged her down onto the couch in the living room, or when he disappeared into the kitchen and returned with the tea that she'd forgotten all about.

"Thought you liked coffee, not tea," he said, taking her hands and wrapping them around the ceramic mug as he sat on the wrought-iron coffee table, facing her. "But you've obviously just fixed this."

He'd removed the tea bag, she realized dimly, staring into the pale liquid. "I stopped drinking coffee," she said faintly. "You're really serious about all this." She lifted her gaze to his.

His expression was solemn. "Yeah."

Her brother's words echoed in her head. "That's the only time Sloan's spoken directly to me in three years." She lifted the mug, but lowered it again without drinking. "We used to live together, you know. We shared a brownstone." The first place she'd really called *home*. But even that hadn't lasted. "I didn't think there was anything about each other that we didn't know. Then he decided to go undercover, and…" She shook her head. "Everything changed. Everything." Her life. Her brother.

"Not forever. Temporarily. That's what you said." Axel leaned forward, his looped fingers hanging loosely between his wide-planted legs. His deep gold hair sprang back from his tanned forehead and his gaze was steady. "This situation—me, here—will be temporary, too."

Of course it would be.

Because his interest in her had nothing to do with their time in Braden and everything to do with his job.

She cleared her throat, but the knot there seemed destined to remain forever. "So…say I *do* go along with all of this—" which she wasn't saying yet, no matter how shocking it had been to hear Sloan's voice "—what can I expect? I mean, what do you plan to, um, to do? Follow me when I go to the grocery store? Stand guard outside the shop when I'm open? What?"

"Stay with you around the clock. There will be some periods when I can't be with you. That's when my backup will be in place."

"Hold it." She waved her hand and set her mug on the neat pile of magazines beside the muscular bulge of his jean-clad thigh. "Go back to this clock issue."

"What about it?"

She had a fleeting image of an armed guard standing on the front step of her shop, scaring away customers.

Just because her life in Weaver was supposed to be temporary didn't mean that she could afford to lose business. Classic Charms was no front. It was a real business. One that she'd worked hard to make successful. It kept her ancient house in decent repair, and now more than ever, she needed the shop to remain as profitable as it possibly could to tide her over when the baby came.

"I can't have you hanging around my shop every minute that I'm open." People would get the wrong idea. They'd start putting one and one together, and getting three.

"Not just the shop. Here, too. 24/7."

Could this possibly get any worse? "For how long?" Her voice rose despite her efforts.

"Until we neutralize the threat against Sloan."

"We?"

"The authorities. Hollins-Winword. Your brother."

"But not you?"

"That's not my assignment."

She managed not to wince again. "And how long will this *neutralizing* take?"

His fingers spread, palms turned up. "As long as it takes."

She pressed her fingers against her forehead, her headache growing by the minute.

*As long as it takes.*

How many times had her father used that line, when he was moving them to yet another home? Another state? Another country?

*How long would they get to live here this time?* she would ask, forever hoping that it might be long enough to finish a school year. Make a friend. Set some roots.

All the things she'd longed for since before she could remember.

Her father's impatient answer had always been the same. "We'll be here as long as it takes, Tara." Then he'd send her away to bug her mother, because whatever he was doing behind the closed doors of his office—he'd always had an office, no matter how tiny a place they had—was far more important than answering the questions of his only daughter.

She couldn't remember how many moves it had been before she'd stopped asking.

But she *had* stopped.

And when she'd been old enough, she'd made her *own* home. Set down her own roots.

Only to give it all up again when Sloan had asked her to.

"Couldn't someone else do this—" she said as she waved her hand, grimacing "—guarding business?"

"Someone else could. But someone else isn't. I am."

She wanted to toss her hands out and cry "Why?" but she did no such thing. "People are going to…to get the wrong impression if they see you dogging every step I make. Particularly after being at the dance together...and...and what you told Joe Gage. You didn't even go over to say hello to your own family because we were dancing. You know how gossip thrives in this town. Everyone will be talking about us!" The very idea of it was enough to give her hives.

His eyebrows rose a little and she tried not to notice the way his gaze seemed to drop for a burning moment to her mouth. "Would you rather people gossip about our involvement—" he said as he sketched in the air quotes around the word "—or know the real reason we're together?"

"I don't like giving people a reason to gossip about me at all!"

"They already gossip about you."

"No they don't," she disagreed.

He made a disbelieving face, slanting his head. "Yeah. They do. But maybe they wouldn't be so anxious to do so if you didn't act so standoffish toward everyone in town."

Indignation weighted down her jaw. "I'm not standoffish! I talk to every customer at the shop. I serve at all the civic events, just like all the other business owners do."

"That's business. What about friends? I know you don't have any lovers."

Her face went hot. Aside from her brief, lamentable excuse of a marriage when she'd been eighteen, she'd had no lovers but Axel—information which she'd foolishly shared with him during "that" weekend. "I *did* go to the dance this evening," she reminded him. "Not that my friends *or* lovers are your business."

"It is my business when I need to know who's in your life." He lifted his hand, forestalling her further indignation. "But it doesn't matter. I already know the basics. Tonight's dance aside, you don't socialize, Tara. You go to rotary and chamber of commerce meetings. You don't even stay to drink a cup of coffee and complain about the pastor's sermon when you go to church on Sundays."

She tightened the edges of her robe over her bare knees, feeling stiff as a poker. "What makes you so certain of that? Because you listen to the *gossip* about me?"

He sighed again. "Hollins-Winword set you up here in Weaver in the first place. Do you think nobody has been keeping an eye on you since then?"

Her jaw loosened and she pushed off the couch, blinking through the abrupt head-rush from standing so quickly. "You've been…been *spying* on me? You knew all of this…this stuff when you and I…when we—" She broke off, unable to form words for the outrage filling her veins.

"Nobody's spying on you. And when I ran into you in Braden, all I learned about you, came from you. But the agency has kept an eye out for your safety since you moved to Weaver. That would have included vetting anyone who seemed to be getting close to you. Only nobody did."

*Except him.*

Her otherwise utterly solitary lifestyle wasn't just something noticed behind her nosy neighbor's twitching lace curtains at the front windows.

It had become notations in someone's logbook.

Humiliation burned inside her, keeping company with the hovering nausea and the ulcerating worry about her brother. "So who's been prepared to do this *vetting?*" She nearly choked over the word. "And did they vet *you?*"

"Nobody knows about us but us, which under the circumstances is just as well." He pushed to his feet, and it was more like an uncoiling of a dangerous animal. "I know this is hard to hear. If it weren't for the latest threat against your brother, there would've been no reason for you to know that anything out of the ordinary was even going on."

"No reason? No reason to know that someone," she threw her arm out toward the front door, "is out there watching my life, tallying up my activities in neat little columns?"

"Think of it more like you've had some guardian angels watching over you."

She gave a short, humorless, laugh. "Pretty words for an unacceptable situation. How would you like it if you learned that someone was *watching* over you?"

He had the decency, at least, to grimace. "I wouldn't," he admitted. "And there's nothing to be gained by debating a moot point. You know now. So let's get the details of my watch worked out. You open the shop every day except Sunday?"

"Yes," she answered, grudgingly. "And I haven't agreed to anything."

"I don't need a lot of space here," he continued on, as if she'd said nothing at all. "I can sleep on the floor, if need be."

Her hands curled. "If you're expecting an invitation to use my bed, you can forget it," she said witheringly.

His jaw cocked slightly to one side. "I'm your bodyguard. It would be inappropriate to share your bed."

She yanked the sash of her robe tighter. "Then I'm glad we're agreed."

"I didn't say I agreed," he clarified, his voice smooth. "I said it would be inappropriate."

A flush started in her forehead and burned all the way down to her toes. Which annoyed her all over again.

She snatched up the mug and carried it into the kitchen.

"The situation won't be as bad as you think," he said, following her.

No. The situation was worse than *he* could possibly think.

She dumped the tea down the sink and rinsed the mug. She wanted coffee. Or something a heck of a lot stronger.

She turned and leaned back against the counter. "How many people know you're not really a horse breeder?"

"I told you. I *am* a horse breeder."

"Fine. How many people know about the other—" she said as she waved her hand "—you know. Secret stuff."

She hated secrets.

The irony that she was keeping a pretty large secret herself wasn't lost on her.

"Very few. It's important to keep it that way."

"Why?"

"Hollins-Winword does a lot of good work. But in the process, they've made plenty of enemies."

She plucked at a loose thread on her sleeve. "So, it benefits *you* that everyone thinks you're sticking to me like glue because you're suddenly infatuated with an older woman."

That dimple beside his cheek flashed momentarily. "You're barely two years older than me. That hardly makes you a cougar, darlin'."

"My name is Tara." *Darlin'* was for the man who she'd believed wanted to share her bed as badly as she did. Who'd made her actually think about a future.

His faint smile threatened to widen and she wished she'd kept her mouth shut.

She turned and yanked open the refrigerator. It was well past dinnertime; she needed to eat. But nothing appealed, particularly with the way her stomach seemed to be rolling around. "So, I suppose your behavior at the dance tonight was just to set up the pretense that you and I are involved." She addressed her comments toward the jug of milk.

"We are involved." His hand closed over the back of her neck and she jerked, shoving the refrigerator door closed as she turned so his hand would fall away.

"No, we are *not*," she snapped. One weekend did not an involvement make and she'd do well to remember that. "If anything, this is just going to look suspicious to people. Seeing how—as you've observed—my life has always been so sterile. And then you come to town and boom, we're an item?" She shook her head, dismissively. "Who's going to believe that?"

The corner of his lip cocked upward. "They know me."

She grimaced. "What? No skirt goes unchased?"

"Not at all. Just that people who know me, know that when I set my eye on something—or someone—I don't pussyfoot around. I act." He paused a beat and the air between them was suddenly thick. Hot. "You, of all people, should be aware of that."

She shut off her reaction before the erotic images could leap out of the cage where she'd kept them locked since waking up, alone, in that motel room. "I prefer not to talk about that."

His eyes seemed to turn even more golden. "Not talking about it doesn't mean it didn't happen, darlin'."

She couldn't possibly be more aware of that fact, all things considered. "That weekend was an…anomaly. Obviously. It's not something that's going to be repeated."

"You're right," he agreed. "As long as I'm your bodyguard."

Unfortunately, she wasn't entirely certain how to take that. All she knew was that there were butterflies whisking through her veins that she couldn't attribute to her fear for Sloan no matter how badly she wanted to.

She slid out from between Axel and the scarred butcher block countertop, moving far enough away so she could breathe again without danger of inhaling his oddly intoxicating scent. "Fine. I'll do this for my brother. But that's the *only* reason."

Axel's head tilted slightly. "Fair enough."

## *Chapter Five*

He'd won a battle, but Axel knew that wasn't exactly winning the war. Which is what Tara's resistance pretty much felt like.

Leaving her in the kitchen, he went out to his truck to bring in his gear. He dumped his duffel bag on the floor next to the couch and after exploring every room under her baleful and silent gaze, he went back outside, getting a lay of the land there, too.

The neighboring houses with porch lights casting beams over snowy front yards. The few vehicles parked in snow-covered driveways. The dog barking about two doors down.

Weaver was his hometown; as comfortable to him as his favorite pair of boots. It didn't matter if he was gone for months or years at a time. When he came home, he still knew what—who—belonged. And didn't belong.

Satisfied that all was as it should be, he went back inside.

"I don't see why your truck has to be out here for all of

God and country to see," she complained the moment he shut the door behind him.

"So that God and country *can* see it," he reminded her. He pulled the enamel doorknob and locked the door. "You need deadbolts on your doors." On his survey, he'd seen a door at the rear of the house in the kitchen, leading to an unfenced backyard. Hardly ideal circumstances—though he knew from experience that a fence would do little to keep out a determined person.

Without comment, she headed through the living area and down the short hall, presumably to the one bedroom that was actually set up as a bedroom. The second room, he'd discovered, was outfitted with two modern work surfaces and a sizable shelving unit full of orderly plastic bins.

When she returned, he was studying the magazines stacked in the center of her wrought-iron coffee table. "They're all about jewelry making," he said aloud, fanning the neat pile out like giant playing cards.

"I have to get ideas from somewhere or the display cases at my shop would be pretty bare."

"You make the jewelry you sell in your shop?"

"Most of it. And why are you surprised?" Her smile was humorless. "Aren't you and your logbook keepers supposed to know everything there is to know about my life?"

"I'm just surprised you didn't tell me about it in Braden."

Her expression closed and she headed to the large picture window, reaching for the wand to adjust the plantation shutters closed across it.

"It's better to leave them closed."

Her hand hung in midair for a moment before she finally lowered it. She turned away from the window.

He sighed at the sight of her increasingly drawn expression. "I'm sorry."

"But it's the way it is, isn't it?" She didn't look at him as she leaned over and squared up the edges of the magazines that he'd un-squared. The silky strands of her hair slid forward, baring the tender nape of her neck for the briefest of moments.

Plenty long enough, though, for his gut to tighten.

He'd kissed that very spot of silky smooth, pale skin.

And had been reliving the experience almost every night since in his dreams.

He cleared his throat and looked away, only to get distracted by the bare ankles peeking out below the hem of her enveloping robe. "We didn't stay long enough to have dinner at the dance. Are you hungry?"

"No." She didn't look at him. "If you are, then I suppose I can fix something."

He felt starved, and not just for food. "I don't expect you to cook meals for me."

"Good. And I expect you not to use up the hot water if you shower before I do in the morning."

His mind took an eager side trip down the lane paved with the memory of her and him and a shower. With an effort, he reeled it in.

She went into the kitchen and he followed.

Already, she was pulling pans out of a lower cupboard and was reaching for the refrigerator. She pulled a thick glass jar from the fridge and set it on the counter. "Pasta's in the upper left cupboard."

He took the hint and opened the cupboard. The inside of her ancient cabinet was organized to the nth degree.

He took down the tall spaghetti container. "I thought maybe you were exaggerating when you told me that you alphabetized your CDs and books and DVDs." Judging by the cabinets, he realized she hadn't been.

"I like order."

She'd told him that, too, when he'd teased her about remaking the motel bed before pulling her back down onto it and unmaking it all over again. "What else can I do?" He'd try anything as long as it would distract his one-track mind. She was pulling fresh vegetables out of the refrigerator. "Wash? Chop?"

She gave him a narrowed look. "Wash and chop what?" She held up a zucchini. "These?"

"I do have a mother," he reminded her drily, and plucked the squash out of her hand before she could protest. "She did her best to house-train me. Sliced or diced or what?"

Her espresso-brown eyes were full of suspicion. "Sliced."

She had a fancy knife rack that his mother would envy and he selected a knife. "Cutting board?"

She pulled out a wooden board fashioned in the shape of an enormous apple and put it on the counter near the deep, farm-style sink. She set several other vegetables on the counter next to it. "Wash them first."

He'd already turned on the tap. "Yes, ma'am," he drawled, more than a little amused at the way she stood there, watching. As if to be certain that he knew what he was doing when it came to rinsing a few vegetables. "You want any of this stuff peeled?"

"No. Just sliced."

She continued watching him. It was enough to make a guy all thumbs, but he managed to slice the zuke without slicing any fingers and he looked over at her. "I am capable of slicing a few vegetables without spilling blood."

She flushed a little. "I've never seen a man working in the kitchen before." Her discomfort was palpable. "Aside from a restaurant chef or on the cooking channel."

"Never? Not your dad? Your brother?" Their families and their pasts were things they hadn't talked about in detail when they'd secluded themselves with only each other, a chocolate cake, a box of condoms and pizza delivery.

She stuck out her chin. "My father believed the kitchen was my mother's domain. It seemed to be an idea that Sloan inherited. The only thing I ever saw him do for himself in the kitchen was toss a bag of popcorn in the microwave and hit the start button."

Axel picked up a fat red bell pepper and whacked it in half, cleaning out the seeds. "You've met my mother. You think she'd raise a son who couldn't find his way around a kitchen?" He almost laughed at the idea of his accountant mother giving any child of hers some slack. "I probably spent more time in the kitchen with my mom than my sister, Leandra, did. *She* didn't learn how to boil water until she went off to Europe to work on the production crew of some guy's cooking show."

Tara had sidled closer and was leaning against the scarred butcher block counter. "Are you close?"

He shrugged, all the while noticing the fascination in her expression that she would probably deny if he pointed it out. "Yeah, I suppose so. All the Clays are pretty tight. Brothers. Sisters. Cousins."

At least they had been.

He tamped down on the dark thought. "What about you?" He turned the question back on her. "What's it like being a twin?"

Her long, silky lashes immediately lowered, shielding her eyes from him. "I don't know what it's like not being a twin." She turned and picked up the large pot she'd pulled from the cupboard and busied herself with filling it with water.

She gave no further glimpses of fascination about the dynamics of his family—which seemed plainly different from her own. Not while they finished preparing the meal. Not as they sat at the small wrought-iron table situated in the bay window on the other side of the kitchen. Not even when they cleaned up afterward. He was pretty certain that seeing him with his hands plunged in soapy dishwater was just as unusual to her as had been his minimal deftness with the knife and chopping block.

It was late by the time they were finished and she snapped

off the light in the kitchen, shooing him to the living room. "My second bedroom is my workroom," she said abruptly. "You'll have to make do with the couch." She waved toward it as if he couldn't see, perfectly well, for himself.

"I've made do with worse," he commented.

A furrow formed over the bridge of her sharply defined nose. She closed her arms around her waist and walked across the room. Clearly putting distance between them.

"H-how often have you had to do this sort of thing?"

He didn't ask for clarification. "I'd have to sit down and count."

"That many?" She moistened her lips. "Have they all ended well?"

"Not all," he admitted and hoped that he wouldn't have to elaborate.

"How long have you had to spend on one—" she asked as she waved her hand. Again the long folds of her robe swayed just enough for Axel to glimpse her ankles.

"—case?" he provided, dragging his gaze up to her face to see her nod. "Six months was the longest."

She paled and he lifted his hand. "I don't think that's what we're looking at here," he added quickly.

She seemed only slightly relieved. But she wouldn't have been even the least bit relieved if he'd told her why he thought what he did.

That if they didn't nail the person, or persons, out to get Sloan ASAP, her brother probably wouldn't live to see the next six months.

"I'm gonna check around the house again. Keep the door locked."

She gave him a questioning look. "Check for what?"

"Anything out of place." He grabbed up his jacket and went to the door, stepping out. "Lock it," he told her through the door when he failed to hear the lock being set.

After a moment, he heard the soft *snick.*

Exhaling a cloud of vapor that glistened in the faint gleam of the porch light, he checked around the house. His footprints from earlier were the only ones in the snow, showing quite clearly how he'd paused at each window, each door.

A slow-moving sedan was pulling close to the curb behind his truck, the driver's mop of curly blond hair recognizable in the dim light even before Dee Crowder rolled down her window and waved at him. "You disappeared pretty quickly from the dance," she called out to him. "Everything all right?"

He headed toward her car. Nobody better than Dee to continue the gossip rolling around town that he was shacking up with the lovely, local shop lady.

"Just fine." He ducked down to see her through the window. "We weren't really looking for a crowd."

Dee's smile fizzled a little. "I didn't realize you knew Tara that well."

He was vaguely sorry that her feelings might be dented, but there'd never been anything between him and the teacher. Never any suggestion that there would be.

He glanced at Tara's house, seeing the slight angle in the shutters at the window.

Despite what he'd told her about keeping the shutters closed, she was watching from inside the house.

"Knowing each other better is something we're working on," he said as he looked back at Dee with his typical Axel grin.

"I see." Dee drew her head away from the opened window. "Well, I'd better get home. It's late." Her voice was conscientiously chipper. "Nothing like a lot of dancing to wear a girl out. You and Tara have a good night."

"Thanks, Dee." He ducked his head down a little more, looking in at her. "Drive carefully, okay?"

"Oh, I'm always careful," she said airily, and pulled away

from the curb. He watched long enough to see her turn into a narrow driveway about four houses down, and returned to the house.

Tara pulled open the door when he reached it. "How'd you explain all this to Dee?"

He flipped the lock after him. "Not much explaining necessary when she sees me parked in front of your house at this hour."

She looked disbelieving. "Why didn't you just tell her the truth? She's your…friend, isn't she?"

"She's my cousin's coworker," he corrected, shrugging out of his jacket again and tossing it over the arm of the couch for lack of someplace better.

"Looked pretty friendly to me to be a coworker, cousin-removed."

He wiped the grin off his face before it had a chance to form. "Dee's a friendly girl."

"She's a flirt."

The grin was a little harder to keep contained. Tara was showing all the earmarks of being jealous, and enjoying that was not going to earn him points.

Nor was it going to make his job here any easier, if he couldn't keep his focus strictly on the task at hand.

"Flirt or family friend, it doesn't matter. We—" he said as he wagged his finger between his chest and her "—stick to the cover."

Her lips pursed softly, which only succeeded in drawing his attention to them. "You'd lie to your family?"

"I'd lie to anyone if it meant keeping you safe." He deliberately looked away and sat down on the deep couch upholstered in some smooth, brownish-colored stuff.

It was a little short on length for his taste, but it was soft and comfortable, which was a bonus for him since most of her floors were covered in hardwood, save a few large area rugs beneath the furniture. He hadn't been joking about being prepared to sleep on the floor, but a decent couch would be welcome.

The wide four-poster bed of hers would be even better.

He ignored the voice in his head and began pulling off his boots. "What's going to draw the attention of someone more? The gossip that you and I are hitting the sheets, or the gossip that you need a bodyguard?"

"Nobody in Weaver would ever need a bodyguard."

His boot came free and he dropped it on the floor. "Exactly. That kind of talk we definitely don't want."

"But to lie to your family—" she said and just shook her head, looking thoroughly disapproving. "How will they forgive you when they find out?"

They'd get over it where Tara was concerned, because they'd understand how his job worked.. How could they not, when all he'd done was follow in his old man's footsteps by joining the agency? If there was one thing the Clays understood, it was allegiance to the agency.

It was the other lie that he was afraid they'd find unforgiveable. About Ryan. Allegiance to the family was an entirely different matter.

He yanked off his other boot and dumped it beside the first. "They'll adjust."

"Right." Her voice was three shades too calm. "Because that's what families have to do." She headed for the hall. "I'll get you a blanket and pillow."

Considering how delighted she was about his reason for being there, he was glad for the offer. Instead of blocking him every minute of the day while they were alone, at least she was making an effort to be cordial. Dinner. Some bedding.

What more could a guy want?

She padded on her silent, stocking feet back into the living room, bearing a long pillow, a crisply folded sheet, and an ancient-looking quilt. She set it all on the coffee table and the lapel of her robe gaped enough to give him a glimpse of the hollow at the base of her throat.

He could want a helluva lot more.

"I know the quilt looks old, but it's one of the warmest blankets I have."

"Looks like half the quilts my mom's got on the beds at the farm. All put together by great-grandmothers or someone."

If she noticed the sudden hoarseness in his voice, she ignored it. "I bought that one at an estate sale a few years ago. If it was someone's great-grandmother who stitched it, it wasn't mine." Unsmiling, she tugged at the sash around her waist again, tightening it. "Is there anything else you need?"

Other than for her to look at him without loathing him for leaving her in Braden the way he had? "I'm good. Thanks. I'm not here as your guest. I don't need entertaining. You can go to bed if you want." He was running on too little sleep, himself, thanks to the time difference between Wyoming and Bangkok, where he'd failed at convincing Ryan to come with him.

"All right." She looked distinctly uncomfortable but was trying to hide it. "Good night, then."

"G'night, Tara."

After a hesitating step or two, she practically ran out of the room. A few seconds later, he heard the firm sound of her bedroom door closing.

He exhaled and leaned back against the couch, raking his fingers through his hair and pressing the heels of his palms against his sleep-deprived eyes.

He was tired enough to sleep for a week straight. Even *with* the tormenting image of Tara sliding into bed with only a few inches of plaster and paint between them.

But instead of spreading out the bedding she'd provided him, he pushed it further to one side, dislodging the tidy magazines again. Then he pulled his laptop out of his duffel bag and set it on the coffee table, flipping it open and powering it up.

In seconds, he was logged in to Hollins-Winword's tightly secured site. He entered the day's report, grimacing as Tara's words about having her activities entered in someone's logbook haunted his mind.

He signed out, and was ready to close the computer down again when his fingers paused over the keyboard. Even though he knew the one message he wanted to see wouldn't be there, he logged in to an equally convoluted server and checked his e-mails.

Offers to improve his sexual prowess. Pleas to send money to aid foreign royalty suddenly thrown into impoverished circumstances. Junk mail galore.

But no message from Ryan.

He closed down the computer again and leaned wearily against the couch.

The one thing he'd wanted to accomplish as an agent for Hollins-Winword was to prove that his cousin was alive.

But now that he'd done so, there wasn't one damn thing he could do about it but keep the truth from everyone else.

## *Chapter Six*

Despite her fear that she wouldn't sleep a wink with Axel under her roof, Tara did.

The second her head hit the pillow, she was out and she didn't wake up again until sunlight seeped through her bedroom window.

She pulled the robe on over her pajamas and when she didn't hear any noise coming from the living area, she crept to the bathroom, closing the door with care before opening the squeaky medicine cabinet to get her toothbrush.

The large bottle of prenatal vitamins sitting on the second shelf greeted her.

She snatched the bottle off the shelf and shoved it in the side pocket of her robe. As she finished brushing her teeth, she didn't look at herself in the mirror, afraid guilt would look back at her.

Then she flipped on the shower over the claw-footed tub and waited the usual eternity for the water to warm.

Having Axel under her roof felt much too intimate, and they weren't even being intimate. Not now. Not anymore.

The memory of that weekend, however, was as hauntingly brilliant as if it had been yesterday.

She shrugged off her robe and pajamas and stepped into the tub, turning her face directly into the shower spray as if it could flood the thoughts into nonexistence.

On that score, the water failed miserably.

She emerged a short time later squeaky clean, but no less disturbed. She dragged a comb through her hair, pulled on her robe again and cautiously stepped out into the hall.

"Good morning."

She nearly jumped out of her skin at Axel's deep voice. "I thought you were still sleeping." Instead, he was sitting at the small table in her kitchen where he had a direct line of vision down the hallway to the bathroom.

"Been awake awhile. I brought in your newspaper. It snowed during the night."

She glanced toward the window behind him, but naturally, the shutters were drawn closed.

He lifted the off-white mug from the table where it was sitting next to a laptop computer and the Sunday paper. "You're out of coffee."

He looked disgustingly awake for a man who'd slept on a couch that was at least a foot too short for him. The only concession she could see to the night that had passed was the shadow blurring his hard jaw and the chambray shirt that he'd pulled on but hadn't buttoned.

"I told you. I stopped drinking it." She was abrupt. More from the effort of not staring at the slice of hard chest revealed by his loose shirt than from her present coffee embargo. She'd had to get rid of all coffee from her house just to keep from drinking the stuff that her obstetrician had cautioned against.

Secrets were a pain in the rear. They always had been and

she'd never been good at keeping them. Something her father had pointed out whenever she'd let slip that he worked for the CIA.

"Then why keep the fancy coffeemaker?"

"It was a gift from Sloan," she said truthfully. He'd given her the machine when they'd bought the brownstone in Chicago. "If you want coffee we'll have to pick up some. It won't bother me." She had some willpower, after all.

Her gaze drifted back to his chest with its soft whorl of hair that was darker than the thick hair springing back untidily from his forehead. Her mouth was very nearly watering—something she would have rather blamed on their talk about coffee. She turned and headed toward her bedroom.

The bottle of vitamins in her pocket rattled and she nearly cringed, closing herself quickly in her room to exchange the robe for a pair of jeans she could no longer fasten at the waist, and a fleecy tunic that successfully hid that fact.

She would have liked to have hidden longer in her room, but she refused to behave like a coward. She was *over* the man.

She'd ignore the pounding in her heart and the current in her nerves. Pretend none of it existed, and before long, pretense would become reality.

She had ample reason for wanting that reality.

Axel Clay was the most unsuitable man she could have chosen. He'd walked away from her without a backward glance and was only here now because of his job. A job whose danger and secrets she wanted to keep far, far away from her child.

Growing up with a father whose life revolved around secrets was no life for anyone.

So she left the bedroom, going straight to the front window where she slanted the shutters enough to look outside, not caring whether he'd chastise her or not. Fresh snow blanketed the ground.

She went to the coat closet and pulled out a red knit cap to cover her damp hair. A little snow shoveling would do her good.

"Had you figured for the type who stuck to the Sunday-best rule." Axel was still sitting at the table. "I was even going to polish up my dress boots for the occasion."

"I'm not going to church today."

His eyebrows rose. "You go to church every Sunday."

Did he know that because of the logbook, or because he remembered her telling him that when they'd been lying in that motel room while they fed each other cold pepperoni pizza? "I'm not going today."

"Why?"

She pulled out her parka and shoved her arms through the sleeves. "Because I assume you'd insist on accompanying me. And I'm not up to sitting through a worship service where we'd be pretending to be involved." She yanked up the zipper.

"Okay. But people might assume that we're here doing something else more…entertaining. All that folderol yesterday at the gym aside, *today* is Valentine's Day."

She went hot and couldn't blame it all on the parka. "Fine." She pulled the zipper right back down. "I'll go get dressed." She marched right back down the hall and slammed the bedroom door behind her.

She pressed her palm against her pounding heart. So much for pretending she didn't care.

She changed clothes again, slipping into a red pantsuit with a loosely swinging jacket that nearly reached her thighs. She ran the blow dryer over her hair, dashed on a little mascara and lip gloss and went back out to the kitchen. "Well?" she asked when she found him still sitting at the table. "Are we going, or not?"

"Going." He closed the computer on whatever he was doing and rose. His shirttails flapped apart as he stood, baring even more of his chest and a hard, ridged abdomen. "Give me five minutes."

He moved past her to head down the hall to the bathroom. Within seconds, she could hear the pipes rumbling as he turned on the shower.

She would have to turn her eyelids inside out to erase the images her memory painted there.

Instead, she gulped down a quick glass of milk and was glancing through the Sunday paper when he emerged. His hair was water-dark and slicked back from the strong lines of his face. He had a towel slung around his neck. Water droplets were sparkling on his shoulders, slipping down his spine toward the denim at his waist. He bent over to rummage in the duffel bag that was still sitting on the floor by the couch.

He pulled out a shirt and held it to his nose. Made a face and wadded it back up, shoving it right back into the bag. "We'll be going out to the Double-C later this afternoon for Sunday dinner. There'll be a mountain of food. Always is no matter how much of the family shows. So, if there is anything you want to get done before we drive out there, let me know now." He extracted a thick, ivory sweater and shook it out. "We'll take care of it after church."

"Sunday dinner?" Her voice was faint. "I don't think so. If you need to go, then go, but I'll stay here."

He rose again, dropping the sweater on the couch before he dashed the towel over his shoulders and chest with no hint, whatsoever, of self-consciousness.

And why would there be? The man was built better than a Greek god, for pity's sake.

"Is there something about '24/7' that you don't understand?" He tugged a white T-shirt over his head, then reached for the sweater.

"Why would you want me—and all the danger supposedly surrounding me—around your family?"

"There's not much of a safer place than being around my

family. I have to go. Which means you have to go, too, interested or not."

Her jaw set. "I don't *have* to do anything," she reminded him.

He sighed noisily. "Right. But you will because somewhere in that pretty, stubborn head of yours is a wide streak of common sense. If there weren't, we wouldn't even be here having this discussion. You'd have told me to take a flying leap even after you heard from Sloan. You'd have told me that you could handle whatever life—and your brother's case—threw at you."

Her chest felt tight. "But I don't want to go!"

"Why not? You told me that you dreamed, one day, of having a family to gather around for good old-fashioned family dinners."

"I don't want to talk about what happened—what we said—in Braden!"

His eyes narrowed, studying. "It's just a Sunday dinner. Nothing to get your drawers in a knot over."

"When this is all over with, I still have to live and work in this town. I'd just as soon not give your family cause to hold anything against me."

"I'm not planning to sit down over roasted chicken and mashed potatoes and announce that I'm insanely in love with you. I'm not planning to say anything. It's just a meal and it's hardly been restricted to family and beloved, so relax." His head slanted slightly and it felt as if his brown gaze was peering right inside her. "And you said living in Weaver was temporary. Once this is over, you don't *have* to live and work here at all. So what does it matter to you what people think?"

It mattered because the people he was talking about—his family, all of the Clay family—had never been anything but nice to her.

It mattered, because the people he was talking about were their baby's family.

The underlying layer of nausea that had been her nearly

constant companion every morning for months rippled in warning.

"Fine," she capitulated abruptly. "Warm up the truck."

His eyes narrowed. "Now what's wrong?"

She wanted him out of the house because she was afraid she was going to lose her cookies, despite her empty stomach. "Nothing. I'm just hungry. I'm going to grab a slice of bread." She headed into the kitchen, not waiting for him to respond.

Thankfully, a moment later, she heard the front door open and close. She bent forward, leaning her forehead right against the butcher block and closed her eyes, willing away the nausea.

The last few weeks had been so much better. Her morning sickness had remained in the background. Hovering, yes, but not taking over the way it had at first.

No such luck this morning.

The bread had been a pretense, and she made a dash for the bathroom, slamming the door shut behind her, thanking heaven that Axel was outside at least, so he wouldn't hear her retching.

By the time he came back inside, she was pulling on her coat, feeling immeasurably better, but no happier about the day's planned activity.

Outside, he'd backed his truck into the driveway. The passenger door was already open and she couldn't help but be aware of the way he walked on the outside of her, keeping himself between her and the street.

She didn't speak again until they pulled into the crowded parking lot of the small community church. She recognized nearly everyone who was heading into the sanctuary through the double doors that were thrown wide open despite the winter weather. "What, um, what time do we have to be there this afternoon?"

"Around two. Three." He didn't sound any more enthusiastic than she felt. He parked against the curb near the exit. Where he couldn't get blocked in.

Her father had always done the same thing.

She pushed open the truck door and slid out. He stuck to her side like glue, and when they reached the line of people entering the sanctuary, he folded her hand in his and cheerfully returned the various greetings and speculative looks they received.

She wanted to kick him.

They sat in the rear of the church, primarily because that was the only place there was space, given their last-minute arrival. She could see a few of his family members seated closer to the front. He let go of her hand only long enough to pull a hymnal from the rack in front of him and when more people slid into the pew beside them, he scooted even closer, until she could feel nearly the entire length of him burning down her side.

It was such a preoccupation that she didn't hear a word of Reverend Stone's sermon, and before she knew it, they were singing the last hymn, and people were filing out of the church, heading for the coffee that filled the church with its seductive fragrance.

All too quickly, they were spotted by Axel's family, and though she longed for escape, she could see there would be none. Not for a while.

Axel's father, Jefferson, was the first to reach them. "Too long, boy," she heard him murmur as he clapped his son on the back and then pulled back, taking measure.

Seeing father and son together, the resemblance between the two was even more striking than Tara had realized. The only difference, as far as she could tell, was that the elder Clay's eyes were a brilliant, penetrating blue and his dark-blond hair—scattered with only a small amount of silver—was about six inches longer, and contained in a thick ponytail.

If she'd ever wondered how well Axel would age, she was looking at a spectacular picture of it.

"Tara." Axel's father turned toward her and she felt the full blast of those all-seeing eyes. "It's good to see you."

"And you." She managed what she hoped was a friendly smile, considering that she was practically shaking in her shoes. Not because she was afraid of him. Or of any of the other Clays who were closing in around them, taking up all the space in the aisle between the pews. But because of everything else. Her secret.

"Hello again, dear." Emily Clay squeezed her hand on the way to shouldering between her husband and her son. She reached up and clasped her hands on Axel's cheeks, drawing his face down for a kiss. "*You* are a sight for sore eyes. It's about time we manage to pin you in place for a few minutes!"

If she hadn't been watching closely, Tara would have missed the expression that flickered across Axel's face.

Almost like pain.

For a moment, she managed to forget her own tangled emotions and narrowly prevented her hand from lifting to rest on his back.

Fortunately, nobody else noticed her halted movement as the mass of people who were plainly delighted to see him grew around them.

If she'd had any plans of sliding out of the melee, he quashed them by closing his hand around hers.

So she stood there and smiled until her cheeks ached, turned down the offers of coffee and cookies that kept coming her way and nodded that, yes, they would be at Sunday dinner; until finally Jefferson and Emily headed out, and the onslaught turned down to a trickle. Tara was so relieved when Axel finally pulled her out of the church and hustled her to the truck that she didn't immediately notice that he seemed in as much of a rush to leave as she was.

"You're in a hurry."

"Better not be out in the open for too long."

She swallowed. How on earth could she have let herself forget for even one second what his purpose was?

She looked out the side window and blinked back the stinging behind her eyes. "I need to go by the shop and take care of a few things. Doing the booth at the festival threw off my usual schedule."

"And you're all about being orderly and scheduled."

"Not everything can be like that duffel bag of yours back at the house. Chaos isn't for everyone."

He looked vaguely amused. "Lately, I haven't been anywhere conducive to doing laundry. Maybe my boxers usually have military creases."

She immediately recalled the soft, snug, grey boxers that he'd been wearing beneath his jeans that first night in Braden. Boxers that he hadn't worn for all that long once they'd entered the motel room.

She damned the warmth that rose in her face.

"I have a perfectly good washer and dryer in my basement at home that you're welcome to use. But I'm not tossing your whites in with mine. You can take care of your laundry yourself."

His lips quirked. "Gets under your skin, does it? The idea of your unmentionables swirling around against mine?"

She crossed her arms, looking back out the window again as they traveled the short distance to her shop. He was *trying* to get under her skin and she had no intention of letting him know he was even remotely successful.

She had to keep a distance between them. Period.

"What gets under my skin is a man automatically assuming that laundry and cooking and housework are only the responsibility of a woman."

He turned into the alley behind her shop without prompting. "So along with the no-cooking rule, your dad never picked up a dust rag or knew when to add bleach to a load of whites, either," he assessed. "And once again, you can try painting me with that particular brush, but it's not going to stick." His short laugh curled around her. "Well, maybe a little. I'd rather send the laundry to the cleaners. Money well spent, I've always thought. Particularly since I never mastered that military crease."

Despite herself, she could feel a smile wanting to form. "If there's a military crease in any single thing you wear, I'll eat my hat."

"Dangerous words." He stopped the truck so close to the rear door of the shop that there was barely room for her to get out. Then he turned off the engine and his voice seemed to drop an octave in the silence left behind. "Or don't you remember?"

His insistence on finding the birthday cake for her that unforgettable night.

Her insistence that they'd never find one.

She shimmied out of the truck and fumbled with her door keys before his warm hand plucked the ring out of her fingers and he unlocked the door himself.

She scooted inside but she couldn't get away from the sound of his soft laughter following her, anymore than she could get away from the electricity flooding through her.

Electricity that hadn't cooled one watt since she'd left the Suds-n-Grill with him.

If anything, that particular current was flowing hotter, and brighter, than ever.

## *Chapter Seven*

"We were beginning to wonder if you'd make it or not." Axel's father was the first to notice them later that afternoon when Tara nervously followed a mostly silent Axel into the large main house at the Double-C ranch.

The "big house," Axel had called it as they drove through the iron gate off the highway and approached the rambling stone structure.

Big it most certainly was.

And inside, it was filled with oversized furniture, oversized men and their beautiful families. Those who hadn't been at the church quickly descended on Axel, but this time Tara was able to sidle out of the way, only to come face-to-face with Axel's pixie-sized sister.

"It's a little daunting seeing so many of us in one room," Leandra said with a grin. This time she didn't have her son, Lucas, on her hip the way she had at the festival, but Tara could see the black-haired imp who was the spitting image of his father, climbing up into an old-fashioned wooden rocker.

*Would her baby favor Axel?*

"There are a lot of you," Tara agreed, trying to push away her thought and failing miserably. Was it any wonder, when she was surrounded by prime examples of the family's excellent genetics everywhere she looked?

Thankfully, Leandra didn't seem to notice her preoccupation. "I've learned to let the stampede pass before having my crack at my baby brother." Her eyes were almost the same color as Axel's and they snapped with good humor. "He used to give *me* grief about the time I spent away from Weaver. Turnabout's going to be fair play." She pushed up the sleeves of her closely fitted, ribbed turtleneck. "Is it warm in here or is it me?"

"It's you." Evan corralled his wife with one long arm round her waist. "You're always hot when you're—"

Leandra pinched his arm. "Evan."

His vivid eyes—the same shade that he'd passed on to little Lucas—crinkled. "What?"

She made a face. "Not now."

He shrugged, and slanted his amused gaze toward Tara. Of all the people there, she probably knew Evan Taggart the best, because he, too, was a member of the local chamber of commerce. Not only was he the local veterinarian and Axel's horse-breeding partner, but he and Leandra were the founders of Fresh Horizons, a therapeutic program that brought in young kids from all over the country.

"Did you hear what the final tally was for the blowout yesterday?" he asked Tara.

When he told her, Tara's lips rounded. "Really?"

"Yes, really." Courtney Clay stopped next to them. Her clear, amber-colored eyes were full of laughter. "Thanks to my kissing booth, of course. It's a wonder my lips aren't sprained."

"Too bad you couldn't manage to squeeze a date out of any of those guys the way you squeezed them out of their money," Erik Clay drawled. He was Tristan and Hope Clay's eldest, and while the family resemblance was strong in him, too, he had his mother's violet eyes. "At the rate you're going, you'll shrivel up and die some old spinster."

Courtney lifted her eyebrow. "And when was the last time *you* had a date?" Her voice was dulcet.

Everyone laughed. Even Axel, whose silence on the drive out to the ranch seemed to have passed. He swung his sister right off her feet with one arm, while shaking Evan's hand with the other.

Leandra's laughter was so infectious that Tara couldn't help but smile. There'd never been a collection of family like this in the McCray household and it was impossible to steel herself against the allure.

There was just so much…*love.*

Axel finally settled his sister on her feet. "Why weren't you at church this morning?"

Her eyebrows rose. "Good thing I wasn't. Town's already talking about how crowded it was what with you and Tara practically in each other's laps in the back pew."

Tara's face went hot.

Axel didn't seem to notice, though, as he eyed Leandra with a goading look. "You gaining weight?"

"Trust a brother to point that out," Leandra complained with a wry grimace.

Evidently satisfied that he'd gotten the upper hand again, Axel grinned. "So where's Hannah? Don't see her hiding anywhere around."

Hannah, Tara knew, was Leandra and Evan's adopted daughter and was mildly autistic, though Tara had never seen any particular signs of it whenever she'd come into the shop with her mother. Probably because Hannah had been the inspiration for the program her parents had established. She was practically the poster child for its success.

"Evan's parents have her for the day." Leandra smiled. "Wait until you see her, Ax. She's come *so* far. You'll hardly recognize her."

"I'm looking forward to it." Then Axel turned to Courtney. Tara decided it had to be her imagination the way his smile seemed suddenly strained. "Hey, peanut. So I guess it sounds like they should name the new wing at the school after you for all the kissing you've done, huh?"

She laughed and threw her arms around his shoulders. "God, it's good to have you home." When she pulled back, her eyes looked misty. "It's almost like—" She broke off. Shook her head. "Well. It's just good that you're back where you belong. Selfishly, I hope it lasts for a while this time.

"And *you,*" she said as she turned her head back toward Erik, "need to take a lesson from Ax." Her voice was bright again. "*He* obviously knows how to get himself a date."

It was as if the entire living room fell silent and feeling suddenly like the center of attention, Tara's face went hot. She opened her mouth to protest, but her throat closed up tight. Axel slid his arm over her shoulder and it felt just as proprietary as it had looked when Evan put his arms around *his* wife.

"Damn straight he should know." A gravelly voice cut across the chatter. "Takes after his grandpa, he does."

Tara had only met Squire Clay on a few occasions and could only hazard a guess at his age as Axel's tall, white-haired grandfather stomped through the room. He walked with a cane—a gnarled piece of natural wood—though as far as Tara could tell, he hardly seemed to lean on it.

He stopped in front of Axel, giving his grandson a thorough once-over with his steely blue eyes. "Leastways he's getting a start on the right woman a darn sight earlier than some others I could mention." He swiveled his head around, seeming to give a pointed glare to Jefferson and his other sons, Matthew and Daniel and Tristan. The only one of his sons who wasn't present was Courtney's father—Sawyer, though he had been at the church.

But when Squire looked back at Tara, he gave her a quick, mischievous wink. "If I didn't have a saint of a woman of my own who'd skin my hide, I'd steal you away."

"Go ahead and try." Squire's wife, Gloria, came up beside them, her voice humorously dry. "Then you can be Tara's challenge and I can take a well-deserved rest."

Squire gave her a cantankerous look. "I just called you a 'saint of a woman,' woman. And now you call me a *challenge?*"

His wife looked unfazed as she held up her cheek for her grandson's kiss. The smiling welcome she sent Tara extended from her lips to her blue eyes. "Watch out for these men," she cautioned. "Not a one of my husband's descendents can be trusted when they set their eyes on a pretty girl."

Tara's face flushed all over again. This was exactly what she'd feared. What she'd wanted to avoid.

"Maybe it's Tara who can't be trusted," Axel returned.

"Don't go picking on Tara, now." Emily stepped into their midst. "She's perfectly lovely." She tucked her hand around Tara's arm. "Now, come with me. You'll be safe from all of *them* in the kitchen."

Panic streaked through her and Tara sent Axel a desperate glance, but he was already turning toward his uncles, and she couldn't very well dig her heels into the wood-planked floor and refuse to go with Axel's mother.

Not even if she felt guilt clawing at her.

In the scales of justice, whose lie weighed more?

Axel's intention to let his family think they were involved during the course of this unnecessary business?

Or her failure to reveal that their weekend together in Braden had yielded completely unexpected results?

She had a mental image of the utterly lopsided scale crashing down squarely on her head.

"Look who Axel brought along," Emily said as they entered the spacious kitchen dominated by an enormous oak table.

"What a treat!" Jaimie Clay set a huge, steaming pot on the counter next to the sink and swiped a wave of barely graying auburn hair away from her cheek. "I was meaning to get by your booth at the festival and see if you had any new necklaces, but you'd already left before we got there."

"I do have some new ones," Tara admitted. "If you come by the shop this week, I'm still honoring the sale prices from the festival."

"Honey, as far as I'm concerned, you're not charging enough for your work." Jaimie's voice was dry. "But I'm not above a bargain, so I'll definitely drive into town this week. I'll drag Mags along. She's over visiting Angeline and Brody." Her green eyes twinkled. "Actually, I think Early might be the larger appeal. He's Maggie's two-year old grandson," she provided for Tara's benefit.

Emily laughed, and pulled out one of the chairs at the table. "Can't blame Maggie there. I love watching Lucas, too." She shook her head. "But, oh, for the days when I had enough energy to keep up with a toddler!"

Leandra came into the kitchen, with the little boy in question in her arms. "How much longer before we eat? This guy's getting hungry."

"Here." Jaimie handed the tot a biscuit that she pulled from a large napkin-covered basket.

Lucas latched onto it greedily and shoved half of it into his mouth. Leandra pulled out a chair next to her mother and sank down on it, blowing out a breath.

Emily reached over and took the toddler from her lap. "You're looking flushed."

Leandra shrugged. "Should've worn something cooler than a turtleneck."

"It's Valentine's Day," Jaimie reminded her drily. "There is more than a foot of snow on the ground. How can you possibly be too warm?"

Leandra's lips parted. But no words emerged. Her cheeks turned even pinker as her gaze met Tara's—more in avoidance of her mother's and aunt's, than anything, Tara suspected.

Emily suddenly sat up straighter, earning a protesting squawk from her grandson in her lap. "You're pregnant!"

Leandra groaned. "I *knew* we weren't going to be able to keep it quiet for long."

"It's true then!" Emily quickly slid Lucas into the high chair that was at the table, and grabbed her daughter's face in her hands. "As if you could keep something like that from me for long. That's my grandbaby you're carrying! Do you think I wouldn't know it just by looking at you?"

Tara abruptly moved over to the pot that Jaimie had pretty much abandoned in favor of hugging Leandra. It was filled to the brim with steaming water and boiled potatoes and since there was already a colander in the sink, Tara poured the potatoes into it.

"Oh, honey. I'll get that," Jaimie said quickly.

"I don't mind." Tara would much rather be busy than not, particularly when Axel's mother was rhapsodic over the news about another grandchild.

If she learned about Tara's, though, she might not feel so enthusiastic. Tara and Axel weren't married, after all. Not even close. There was no love. No devotion.

Just one intensely memorable weekend.

"What's all the commotion?" Gloria appeared, with Hope, Courtney and Sarah Scalise on her heels and soon, the kitchen was crammed with even more bodies as Leandra's good news spread.

Sticking well to the background, Tara began mashing the potatoes with the potato masher that was sitting at the ready. But she was painfully aware of Axel's delighted hoot when he joined the throng.

And then Jaimie's husband, Matthew, lifted his head. "What's burning?"

Jaimie rushed across the kitchen, pulling on her oven mitts before drawing a giant casserole pan out of the oven. Suddenly, it was like another tidal wave hit as a dozen hands began assisting to get the meal on the oversized table in the dining room. Axel and Erik were sent back to the kitchen to bring in extra chairs from the table there. High chairs were dragged around and rearranged between various parents and grandparents.

And then, in what seemed like a miracle to Tara, everyone was seated. In the silence that followed, Squire offered a simple blessing that made Tara's throat tight.

But as soon as he passed Amen!, it was as if all hell broke loose again, as dishes were passed, chatter grew louder and bursts of laughter rained down over them all.

Tara couldn't help it. She wanted to sit there and stare and drink it all in.

It wasn't hell, at all.

It was heaven.

"You all right?" Axel's deep voice was soft beside her. Just for her ears.

She blinked, quickly focusing on her plate that through no effort of her own had been filled to the rim. "I'm fine." But her voice was husky and she shored it up with a quick smile. "I'll never be able to eat all of this."

The corner of his lips kicked up. It was, she'd quickly realized, a habit shared by nearly every male at the table. "Sure you will." He lifted his hand and drizzled honey all over the split biscuit hanging perilously near the edge of her plate. "And if you really can't, it's not likely to go to waste around here." He tilted his head pointedly at the way the contents of the serving platters were diminishing at an alarming pace. "I'll finish it."

"You always were a glutton," Leandra said fondly from across the table. "How you manage to keep your 'girlish' figure, I'll never know."

Axel tossed his wadded-up napkin across the table and she dodged it, laughing.

"No throwing at the table," Gloria inserted, without taking her attention from Courtney, who was sitting beside her. From the bits of conversation that Tara could hear, they were thick in discussions about nursing, from which Gloria had evidently retired some years earlier.

"My figure isn't in danger," Axel told Leandra, as she slyly pitched the ivory linen back at him despite Gloria's warning. "Tara's the one with all the food on her plate."

"Honestly, Ax," Sarah chided, shaking her head.

He threw up his hands in surrender. "I'm kidding!" He slanted a look at Tara. "You know that, right? Hell, your figure's about as perfect as any—" He broke off, evidently taking stock of her flaming cheeks. "Okay." He turned square to his plate again. "I'm shoving food in my mouth now."

"Good idea, son." Jefferson's voice was dry.

Everyone laughed. Even Tara managed to join in and just that quickly, the awkwardness seemed to pass—at least where anyone else was concerned.

She, however, was fighting the silly spurt of pleasure and surprise that he'd considered her perfect in any way at all.

She thought she had herself well in control by the time everyone finished eating. And yes, Axel did fork what she couldn't eat onto his plate in a smooth, simple motion that seemed unbearably intimate to her. The second Jaimie rose to clear the table, she hopped up, too.

"I'd tell you to sit because you're a guest, but the more

hands the merrier," Jaimie told her with a grin. "And the quicker we can get dessert on."

"That's what I'm talking about." Squire rubbed his gnarled hands together, looking gleeful.

It was such a modern phrase coming from the old man that Tara had to bite the inside of her lip to keep from chuckling. She gathered the dinner plates that were handed to her as she made her way around the table and she realized she was counting heads as she went. Twenty-two. And that wasn't even the entire family.

"Honey," Emily told Axel, "help Tara with the plates. They're too heavy."

"I'm fine," Tara protested quickly.

Nevertheless, Axel rose, and lifted the entire lot right out of her hands. "You'll learn never to argue with my mother."

"He's right." Jefferson's voice was wry. "It's never gotten me anywhere."

"Oh, shush. Now, Leandra, darling. You haven't said when the baby is due."

Tara quickly retrieved some of the serving ware from the center of the table and started out of the room. "Early July," she heard Leandra answer.

It was all Tara could do not to stop and look at the other woman in surprise. That's when *she* was due, and there was no earthly way she could have gotten away with wearing that skinny, ribbed-knit turtleneck that Leandra had on without showing off her quickly developing baby bump.

She nearly walked right into Axel who was returning from the kitchen. "Want me to take those?"

She stared at him, her thoughts about babies and due dates so front and center in her mind she nearly blurted out the truth right then and there.

And wouldn't *that* be the capper to this boisterous family's Sunday dinner?

"No!" Her answer was a little too emphatic. "No. Thanks. I've got them."

Was it her imagination that his eyes narrowed a fraction? That his gaze became even sharper?

Or was it just her screaming conscience?

She made her feet move and brushed past him, heading into the kitchen where Jaimie was setting out several golden-crusted pies.

"You're a sweetheart," she told Tara. "But don't think you're going to rinse and load the dishwasher."

That was exactly what Tara had been hoping to do. Anything to keep her busy so that she didn't have to go back out and sit among the family.

Only one Sunday dinner with them and she knew she was already in over her head. They were all just too nice. Too perfect. Anything that nice or that perfect would never last. Not from her experiences. "But I—"

"Save it, honey." Jaimie cut her off, looking amused as she wielded her knife over the pies with practiced ease. "It took me about fifteen years to get the point across, but the *men* in this house have to rinse and load."

Tara tucked her tongue between her teeth for a moment, imagining Squire Clay rinsing a dirty dish.

"What you can do, though, is go out and count up the orders for dessert for me. Choices are apple, chocolate silk and pecan."

With no choice, Tara went back into the dining room. Lucas was tugging at his grandfather's thick ponytail. Young Megan and Eli Scalise were squabbling over something while their sheriff father, Max, wiped the squirming hands of his and Sarah's other child, Ben.

She cleared her throat, hoping—and failing—to draw anyone's attention. She tried a little more loudly. "Excuse me." There. At last a dozen heads turned toward her and she cursed the flush that warmed her face. "Jaimie wants to know which pie everyone would like."

Keeping mental tally at the responses was easy until her gaze landed on Axel.

"Chocolate." The way he slowly drew out the word made it seem almost like a caress.

Before heat could run screaming through her veins, Tara turned on her heel and nearly ran back into the kitchen.

But even there she wasn't safe from remembering just how lethal the combination was when Axel Clay was one of the ingredients.

## *Chapter Eight*

"What time do you go into the shop?"

It was the next morning and Tara was standing at her kitchen counter dunking another hated herbal tea bag in hot water while Axel sat at the table with the folded newspaper at one elbow and his computer at the other.

And still she was battling down that surge of hormones that had nearly leveled her the afternoon before.

"I like to be there by eight." She lifted the soaked tea bag by the string. Slowly dunked it again. Anything to keep her eyes off the much-too-appealing man sitting at her table in a ragged gray sweatshirt, jeans and bare feet.

For some reason, she couldn't seem to get her attention off of his feet.

She focused on her tea, but it took an embarrassing amount of effort. "It gives me a little time to get organized before I open at nine."

Except for the past several months when she'd considered

bumping that back at least an hour because that was about how long it took before her wayward morning sickness was battled back under control.

When she'd wakened this morning, however, she hadn't been plagued with nausea. She'd been plagued by a craving that she couldn't afford to indulge.

Axel folded the sports section that he'd been reading. "I'll grab a shower, then, and we can go whenever you're ready."

She made a noncommittal sound. How could she possibly be ready for another non-stop day filled with Axel Clay?

Eyes downcast, she watched from the corner of her vision as those long, bare feet padded toward the living room.

In the quiet, she could hear him rummaging in his duffel bag, footsteps down the hall, bathroom door closing.

She exhaled, dropping the tea bag once and for all. She didn't want herbal tea.

She wanted coffee.

Strong. Blazing hot.

She also wanted sex.

Strong. And blazing hot.

Unfortunately she already knew how well Axel Clay could meet her needs on *that* score.

The pregnancy books really should warn a woman more thoroughly about the hormonal thing.

She ignored the voice inside her head that claimed *Axel* was at the root of the issue, not her pregnancy.

She scrubbed her hands down her cheeks, then dumped the tea down the drain and straightened up the kitchen. She was ordinarily a tidy person. But if she kept putting her frustration into cleaning, before long the old house would be able to double as an operating room.

Annoyed with herself, she left the kitchen. Spotted the tumble of clothing hanging partially over the side of the battered brown leather bag.

Not everything was spotless and tidy.

She looked away from Axel's untidy clothes, straightened the magazines on the table and went to her bedroom.

She could hear the shower running now.

Her imagination went berserk.

She slammed her bedroom door before she did something *really* foolish…like invite herself into his shower.

She was already dressed for a day at the shop in an untucked, blue silk blouse that was slimming without being revealing, and narrow black trousers with a forgiving, elastic waist. She paced around. Straightened the few items on top of her dresser. The mother-of-pearl hand mirror that had been her mother's. A silver-framed photograph of the McCray family when Tara and Sloan had been just five years old. Too young to realize, yet, the kind of lifestyle a child could expect with a father who lived two lives.

She wasn't sure why she kept this particular photograph on her dresser when all of her other family photos—few though they were—were locked in the trunk in the closet. Was it the fact that they'd all looked happy?

She couldn't even remember where they'd been living when she was five. Couldn't recognize the furniture they were sitting on in the portrait, or the stone fireplace behind them, complete with a glowing fire. But her dark-haired mother had looked beautiful and carefree with Tara sitting on her knee and her father had looked handsome and relaxed with Sloan on his.

Or did the photograph merely serve as a reminder about how fleeting that happiness was?

She realized the shower had stopped and looked away from the photograph.

Most days she hardly even noticed the frame sitting there. But "most days" had passed since Axel had returned and complicated everything more by revealing what he really did for a living.

She nearly jumped out of her skin when he knocked on her

closed door. She pulled it open and heat curled through her, low and intense.

The black crew-neck sweater he wore clung lovingly to his torso. His jeans had been replaced by another pair. Just as well-washed. Just as appealing. "You ready?"

*Was she ever.*

"Yes," she said more or less sedately. She glanced down. "You might want some shoes."

He wiggled his bare toes and when she looked up, she caught a faint grin on his face. "Really?" He turned away, heading back into the living room, mercifully missing the shaking hand she pressed to her heart.

She had on her coat if not her emotional armor by the time she reached the front door.

But he stopped her. "Wait. I'll go first." He stomped his foot into the work boot he was lacing. "I haven't been outside yet this morning to check around. I'll tell you when it's okay to come out."

It should have been a needless reminder of the reason why he was under her roof at all, but it wasn't. She swallowed down a ripple of unease. "What if it's not okay?" She didn't like acknowledging the fact that someone might want to hurt her. She *really* didn't like Axel's intention to get between that someone and her if—or when—it happened.

"Stay locked inside, away from the doors and windows, get on your cell and call Hollins-Winword."

"And how would I do that? By calling directory assistance? Somehow I don't think this agency that 'nobody should have to know about' is listed in the yellow pages."

"I programmed the number in your cell phone."

Her lips parted. Unless the phone was connected to the charger in her bedroom—which it usually was at night—the phone was always dumped somewhere in the bottom of her purse. "When did you do that?"

"Yesterday." He reached a long arm for his leather jacket that was tossed over the back of the couch. "Don't worry. I didn't peek through your little black book."

She grimaced. "Funny." He surely knew at this point that there was nothing of the sort in her purse.

She was only grateful that the paperback edition of *After Nine Months* had been relegated to the drawer of her nightstand several days earlier.

Now, she pulled out her cell phone and started to scroll through the numbers, but he'd programmed it to be the very first number. She eyed the digits with surprise. "It's a local number."

"Yeah." Shrugging his jacket over his shoulders, he flipped out the collar and reached for the door.

"Wait!"

He lifted an eyebrow. "What?"

She felt foolish. "What about you? I mean, don't you have a, um, a gun or something?"

His lip quirked and he pressed a hand flat against his chest. "Worried about me?"

"Shouldn't I be? You and Sloan are the ones who insisted there was a reason I *needed* a bodyguard. Do you think I want anyone hurt as a result?"

"Put your conscience to rest, darlin'. This is what I do." He pulled open the door and slipped through.

She darted to the door after he closed it. Her hand hovered over the knob. Her other hand clutched her cell phone.

But she heard nothing from outside. No commotions. No shouts. Nothing, until a car horn bleated twice.

She dismissed her nervousness with a stern exhale and pulled open the door. Shutting it behind her, she locked the brand new dead bolts he'd installed himself when they'd gotten home from the big house the evening before.

He was waiting in his truck, which was once again backed into the driveway, passenger door open.

She lifted her chin, resisting the urge to rush down the steps and dive into the truck. She only felt this way because of Sloan's paranoia.

For five years she'd lived and worked in this community. She refused to be anxious now every time she stepped out of her front door. So she sedately walked to the truck and climbed inside.

It took only a matter of minutes to drive the few miles to her shop. Again he parked alarmingly close to the rear entrance.

Inside, she hung her coat in the back room on the antique iron coat stand, lit a coffee-scented candle, and plugged in her electric teapot while Axel roamed around the front of the shop. She unlocked the safe, removed the till and carried it out front to add to her old-fashioned cash register.

Axel was sprawled on the long leather couch that sat opposite the mahogany bar, which she'd picked up at a fire sale and refinished to use as a counter.

"Too bad you don't have this baby in your living room," he said, tucking his hands behind his neck and crossing his boots at the other end. "It's a lot more comfortable than your couch."

"And two feet too long," she countered. He looked entirely at home on the piece, stretched fully out.

In fact, there'd easily be room for two—

She closed the cash drawer with such a snap that the entire machine jingled. "Drawer sticks," she lied when he gave her a curious look.

"How much is it?"

"Why?" She pulled out a dust cloth and ran it over the counter. "You're not moving it into *my* living room."

He turned on his side, propping his head on his hand. His eyes were full of wicked humor. "Why not? I'm living with you."

"You're *staying* with me," she corrected. "There's a world of difference."

"Yeah." He waited a beat. "No sex."

She snapped out the rag and turned to wipe down the other side of the counter. "That's the way you wanted it."

"I said it would be inappropriate under the circumstances," he returned immediately. "Not that I didn't want…it."

She went hot all over and couldn't manage a suitable response to save her soul.

After a moment, he spoke again. "So, how much?"

She named an outrageous sum.

"Okay. Sold."

She gaped a little and turned to face him. "And just where do you think you're going to put a seven-foot couch?"

"At my place, obviously." He rolled off the sofa in a smooth motion only to lean against the counter, all of two feet from her nose.

His place. The one he'd told her about that weekend in Braden. Built just before he'd left the country and located midway between his parents' house at their horse farm and the Double-C Ranch.

It was torment the way she so easily recalled every word that had passed his lips all those months ago.

"I told you I had only a few pieces of furniture so far," he reminded her. "So do you want a sale or don't you?"

She realized he had a gold bank card tucked between two fingers and argued with her conscience for a while, because the price she'd given him was ridiculously high. "Something this costly should be out of your budget."

His grin widened. "If you want to compare tax returns, I'm pretty sure you'll stop worrying about whether an overpriced couch is in my budget or not."

"If it's overpriced, why want it?"

"Because sometimes I like to get exactly what I want." His gaze dropped to her lips. "And one day, you and I are going to make love on that couch."

She trembled and snatched the card. "In your dreams."

"Definitely," he agreed.

She shoved the card through the credit machine only to realize she had the card backwards and she flipped it around. Ignoring him was close to impossible so she took refuge in the mundane. "How are you going to get the couch there? It took three guys to get it off the truck when it was delivered here."

"I think I can manage the delivery." His voice was dry.

She printed off the charge slip and set it in front of him, along with a pen. "Do I need to see your driver's license as proof of identity?"

His eyes glinted. "I never realized before what a laugh riot you are in the mornings." He added his slanting signature to the slip.

"Hopefully, there won't be many more mornings where you'll have to suffer." She slid the pen out of his fingers and dropped it back into the cheery little clay pot that held her pens. "And we can both get back to our lives."

He folded his arms on top of the counter. His shoulders looked wider than ever as he leaned so close that his lips were only a hairsbreadth from hers. "This *is* my life."

She practically jumped a foot backward so there was no danger that she might sink into that almost-kiss. She tucked the sales receipt into the register drawer. "It isn't *my* life."

She deliberately turned away and went back into the storage room. There were a half-dozen shipping crates she needed to unpack. But before she could display the contents, she'd have to make room in the shop.

Selling the enormous couch would help; she'd have plenty of space then to rearrange the various pieces of much smaller furniture and her clothing displays.

"Why'd you choose to open a store like this when you came to Weaver, anyway?" His voice came from behind her.

"What else was I going to do?" She cast a sideways look at him as she slit open the smallest crate with a box cutter. "The magazine I wrote for was in Chicago."

"What magazine?"

"That detail not in your logbook?" She gave him the name anyway and his eyebrows rose.

"My mom reads that."

"A lot of people read it. Which was one of the reasons I was thrilled to get a position there." She made a face. "*That* lasted all of two years. Now, I'm here."

"Writing is one of those things you can do from a distance, isn't it?"

"Not when you're covering lifestyles in Chicago." She pulled out the protective Bubble Wrap from the box to reveal two small wrought-iron garden tables. She began to lift out the first one.

"Here." He brushed her hands away.

"I can do it."

He ignored her and pulled both tables from the box. "It's not a crime to accept help, you know."

She pulled the cardboard box away and flattened it. "Yes, and when the help goes away, it's easier to have never gotten used to it in the first place." She carried the cardboard to the back door only to stop short and look back at him.

"You're learning." He took the cardboard out to the large bin in the alley that served all of the small businesses in her little strip. He was back in seconds. "So why open a shop, though? Especially one like this? It's not like anything Weaver's ever had."

"Which is why it could have been just as miserable a failure as it was a success," she explained.

"Right." He picked up the squat jar holding the coffee-scented candle. "The smell of this is making my mouth water."

"You can fix some real coffee here." She gestured at the

small coffeemaker sitting on the corner of the desk she rarely used. "Coffee is in the top drawer. I keep it around for the customers." She opened the second drawer of her desk to reveal several boxes. "Crackers and cookies. I usually have a tray by the register with something tempting on it."

"Full-service shopping."

"Something like that." She went to the small sink in the corner and washed her hands. Then she set the crystal tray she used for the edibles on the desk, added a delicate doily to it and began arranging the pretty, imported cookies on top.

"Still, why a shop?"

She tilted back her head, sighing. The man gave "persistence" new meaning.

She added a few more cookies to the tray. "My mother always dreamed about having her own little shop." Talked about it, but could never realize it because they were constantly on the move with Tara's father.

And what was the point of establishing a shop when you'd have to leave it just a few months later?

Axel swiped a little sugar cookie and snapped it off between his straight, white teeth. "Tasty." He popped the rest in his mouth. "You lost your parents when you were pretty young."

It wasn't a question, but she answered anyway. "Twenty." She filled the space he'd made on the tray and carried it out to place it on the counter near the register.

The oversized pendulum clock on the wall said it was still fifteen minutes before opening time, but she slid the "open" sign into place and unlocked the door anyway.

"Now what?" Axel was only a few feet behind her when she turned around again.

"We wait for the customers to flood in." Her voice was dry. Sometimes she went an entire day with only one or two sales.

Fortunately, today, she didn't have to worry about her

profits, thanks to Axel buying the couch. For that matter, she wouldn't have to worry for at least another month.

She stood near the front door, taking in the entire shop with an objective eye so as to decide where to move what after the couch was gone. "I don't suppose asking you to take the couch out now would do any good?"

"Want me out of your hair?" He shook his head. "Sorry. Couch'll wait."

She hadn't expected otherwise. He wouldn't be able to lift it on his own, anyway.

Distraction or not, she'd just have to work around him. She went over to the old-fashioned telephone booth and stepped inside to take down the thin linen and lace chemise that was prominently displayed to replace it with a blue satin bustier.

He tossed himself down again on his purchase. "I still think it's a shame this thing isn't in your house."

"If you're uncomfortable at my house, you know what to do about it." She made the mistake of glancing at him through the glass booth and found her gaze trapped in the intensity of his.

*You and I are going to make love on that couch.*

"Leave," she concluded, sounding strangled.

"I'm afraid I can't do that."

"You didn't have trouble leaving before." The words were out before she could call them back.

His jaw canted a little. "That was unavoidable. Something came up."

She made herself look back at the bustier she was doing a miserable job of hanging. "Business?"

His hesitation was brief. "Yes."

Everything inside her froze.

Because she was absolutely certain that he'd just lied.

## *Chapter Nine*

It was nearly noon before Axel could see the nervous tension finally drain out of Tara's slender shoulders as she busied herself in the brief spaces of time between the customers who came into her shop.

"I can't believe all the sales I've had this morning," she commented yet again as the latest shopper headed out into the cold laden with distinctive shopping bags. They were now alone in the shop. She was sitting on a high, narrow stool behind the counter, thumbing through her sales receipts. "I've never made this many sales in one week, much less one morning."

"Face it. I'm bringing you good luck."

Her smile was pained. "More like people are curious about what you supposedly see in me."

"Anyone with two eyes in their head understands that."

She grimaced and clipped the receipts together before sliding them under the counter, then stretched her arms out behind her.

The motion tightened her blue blouse against the taut swell of her breasts.

He wanted to gnash his teeth together as he made himself look away.

He'd spent most of his time either unpacking crates in the back room, or lending muscle to move displays and racks wherever she pointed. He'd threaded silky, strappy little things onto fancy hangers. He'd folded and refolded tablecloths. He'd run a duster over shelves and turned pots of silk plants, which looked better than real, every which way until she'd been satisfied.

Dozens of ordinary, busywork tasks that weren't responsible at all for him feeling ready to climb right out of his skin.

*That* was owed entirely to the other distractions of the day.

Breathing in her soft, feminine scent every time she moved within two feet of him.

Watching the grace of every movement she made.

Listening to her lilting laughter as she dealt with customers, and feeling jealous as hell because that laughter wasn't for him.

Wanting her so damn badly that he ached all the way to his back teeth.

He moved to the wide, front window and could see Mason Hyde, his backup, sitting in the cab of a nondescript pickup truck across the street. Axel lifted his hand slightly.

Proving himself as observant as ever, Mason opened the truck door and loped across the street. Seconds after that, the bell over the door jingled softly as he entered and doffed his dark brown cowboy hat.

Tara was already looking toward him with her smile ready, but Axel spoke first. "This is Mason Hyde," he introduced. "He'll be my backup."

Alarm touched her face as she looked at the newcomer.

"Ma'am." Mason came toward her, his grizzly-sized hand outstretched. "Nice to meet you."

She shook his hand. "You, too." Her gaze slanted toward Axel. "Is something wrong?"

He shook his head even as Mason offered a quick "No, ma'am." Axel went over to the counter and took one of the few remaining cookies from the tray. It was a pitiful sop to the appetite that was really plaguing him. "I wanted you to meet Mason so you wouldn't worry if you noticed him hanging around the vicinity."

"I tend to rotate vehicles," Mason added. "Don't want anyone taking much notice of me."

"Are you always out there watching from somewhere, then?" Her voice was faint.

"I will be when Axel isn't with you."

She shot Axel another quick look. "You mean you won't actually have to be with me 24/7 after all?"

She looked so hopeful, it was almost deflating. "I'm still staying with you at your place."

"Oh." Her lips closed together.

Definitely deflating. But this was about her safety, not him jonesing for her. "I do have to take care of some business this afternoon, though. Try not to hurt yourself jumping with glee. I'll be back before you close up."

A tiny line came and went between her eyebrows. "Business." She looked at Mason. "Will you be here in the shop, then, Mr. Hyde, or—" she waved her hand toward the window "—just out there somewhere?"

"Just Mason, ma'am. And I'll be out there. But don't worry yourself. I'll never be more than a minute away."

"Keep the back door of your shop locked," Axel commanded.

"I know, I know," she said with some exasperation. "You've told me a half-dozen times already today. And once again, I keep it locked when I'm here, anyway." She slid the cookie platter away from his hand when he started to reach for it and held it, instead, toward Mason. "Would you like some cookies?"

Mason's craggy face split with a genuine smile. "Don't mind if I do. Thanks." He gathered up a handful—in Mason's grip that meant almost every crumb that was left—and headed back toward the door again. "If all goes well, you won't even have to see my ugly mug again." The door jingled softly as it closed behind him.

Tara dashed the cookie crumbs into the small trash container behind the counter. "If you're bored and need an escape, Axel, just say so. You don't need an excuse."

He needed an escape, but not from boredom. "I really do have something to take care of."

"Then go." She waved her hand toward the door only to drop it again when the door jingled and Courtney walked in.

"Should have known I'd find *you* here." Courtney patted his cheek as she stopped in front of the counter. "Give the woman a break, now and then, why don't you? It'll give her a chance to realize that you're not *entirely* annoying and that she misses you."

As long as there was laughter in Courtney's eyes, Axel would be the target of her humor every day of the week and five times on Sunday. "Never thought of that."

"He was just on his way out, actually," Tara told his cousin. "Weren't you?"

The fact that she couldn't wait to get rid of him—however temporarily it might be—felt like a burr under his skin.

He looped his hand around Tara's neck and saw the flare of her widening eyes when he lowered his head and pressed his mouth against hers.

Just for a moment. Not nearly as long as he wanted. Not nearly as deep as he wanted. But just a moment.

A *helluva* moment.

He lifted his head. Smiled into her half-dazed, half-furious face. "I'll be back soon, babe." With a wink at his cousin, he sauntered out the front door.

"Babe," he heard Courtney repeat. "I find it so annoying when a guy calls—" The door jingled, closing off Courtney's indignant voice.

Mason had his head buried under the hood of his truck, looking like a guy with engine trouble. Axel crossed the street some distance away and headed toward the sheriff's station. Only two cruisers and Max's SUV were parked in the adjoining lot.

He went inside and before he even had a chance to open his mouth, the unfamiliar, middle-aged woman at the front desk directed him back to Max's office.

He passed through to his cousin-in-law's office and shut the door behind him. Max was kicked back in his county-issued chair with one boot on the corner of his desk.

"Working hard as usual, I see."

Max grinned. "Somebody's gotta do it. You gonna pay that parking ticket you got the other day?"

Axel pulled out one of the chairs in front of the desk and sat. "Maybe. Your dispatcher send everyone back here without bothering to find out who they are first?"

Max dropped his boot off the desk and sat up. "Julia knows more of the faces in this town than I do," he said wryly. "And has only been in town about a year." He glanced at his watch. "What time were you planning to meet Tristan here?"

"Ten minutes ago. I figured I'd be the one who was late."

The door opened before he'd even finished speaking and his uncle filled the doorway. "You *were* late," Tristan said. He took the second chair. "Max. Appreciate the use of your office."

"Any time." The sheriff rose and sauntered to the door. "But I know how you spy boys like your privacy and I think I hear lunch at Ruby's calling my name."

Tristan waited until the door was closed once again. "I never thought anyone would be as good a sheriff as Sawyer was, but Max is doing fine."

"Why'd you want to meet over here and not at CeeVid?"

Tristan looked grim. "I'm concerned about the security there."

Axel sat up a little straighter. "It's your own company." Nobody was better when it came to security than his uncle was. It didn't matter if it was governmental, Hollins-Winword, or the unrelated video-gaming company Tristan had started on a lark when he'd been younger than Axel was now.

"So you can imagine my pleasure." Tristan seemed to shake it off. "But I'll get that taken care of in time. Right now, I want to know how it's going with Tara."

Axel's antennae went even more finely tuned. "It's going according to book. Which my reports say. Why?"

"Sloan's still concerned."

"He's damn sure shown that by cutting off contact with her all these years." It annoyed the hell out of him. Sloan was Tara's family. Her only family.

And as far as Axel was concerned, family didn't go around hurting family.

Sloan was doing it. Ryan was doing it.

Hell, Axel was doing it by keeping quiet about Ryan.

Tristan's expression didn't change but Axel knew that he'd piqued his uncle's interest, and wished he'd controlled his tongue. If Tristan learned what had happened between Axel and Tara, he'd yank him from the assignment faster than Axel could blink. "I'm not going to let anything touch Tara."

"Despite the phone call you had me set up between them, Sloan's obviously not convinced."

"Tara isn't like Maria. She's not constantly trying to circumvent me." Maria Delgado had, and had paid a fatal price for which Sloan still held Axel accountable. "So tell him to worry about his own skin instead of Tara's. Is there a line, yet, on the hit?"

"Nobody's been able to tie it back to the Deuces," Tristan said. "It's odd, but it doesn't necessarily mean much." His gaze was sharp. "How's it *really* going with her? You two seem…close."

Axel kept his expression easy, but it took an effort. "I wish her schedule weren't so predictable," he admitted. "She's way too accessible."

"A safe house would be better," Tristan agreed.

"But she'd never agree to leave that old place of hers. Or put the shop in someone else's hands. She doesn't think the threat will ever reach her."

His uncle clapped Axel on the shoulder, then stood. "Maybe it won't and no one will be the worse off. In any case, I know you don't need the reminder, but keep your reports confined to the network. And don't make any visits to CeeVid. If you get antsy about location, then damn what Sloan wants. You get Tara out of there, one way or another. Your dad's place. The big house. Even your cabin. They're all better than her place. Sloan would rather have his sister alive and hopping mad, than harmed."

"The trial is supposed to start this week in Chicago. Is McCray there?"

"I don't know where Sloan is," Tristan admitted. "He's gotten too skittish to even tell me. But he's put everything in his life on the line for too long not to see this thing finally be put to bed. He's not going to jeopardize that by failing to testify when he's called, no matter what." He reached for the door and opened it. "Think I'll head over to Ruby's myself. You want to come?"

Axel shook his head and followed his uncle out the door. "I want to get back to Tara."

His uncle just didn't know that Axel's desire went considerably deeper than professional pride.

When they left the station, Tristan walked one direction, heading for the diner and Axel headed the other.

The sky was turning gray as the clouds moved in at a rapid clip. He flipped up the collar of his jacket, jaywalking between the light traffic as he hustled back to the shop.

Inside, it was comfortably warm and smelled of peppermint and coffee.

Tara glanced at him when the door jingled, then turned back to the balding guy she was helping at one of the racks in the corner. Axel had begun thinking of it as the lingerie corner. "What about this one, Tom?" she asked the customer as she pulled out a long, silky-looking nightgown. "Your wife looks at this negligee every time she comes in here. It would make a lovely gift."

Axel leaned against the counter and paged through a magazine that hadn't been sitting there when he'd left. The magazine where Tara had once worked. But he wasn't really interested in the pages of home decorating tips and photographs. Nor was he particularly interested in the red flush rising up the back of Tom Griffin's neck as the man gingerly touched the garment.

"I dunno, Tara," Tom said and then hesitated. "My Janie likes flannel. Been wearing it practically every night since we got married."

"It's your fifteenth anniversary," Tara countered in a gentle, encouraging tone. "I'll bet she'll love getting silk from *you.*"

Tom shot Axel a look that Axel pretended not to notice. "It's not the cost," the other man sort of whispered to Tara. "But it's just awful…well…sexy, dontcha think? What're the kids gonna say when their ma is fixing them breakfast wearing that thing?"

"With the matching robe, it's perfectly modest," Tara assured him just as softly. "But don't think of it in terms of breakfast with the kids. Think of it in terms of a very nice anniversary gift. Trust me, Tom. Janie will love it and she's going to love wearing it for *you.*"

Tom's head turned such a bright red it could have doubled as a train signal.

Axel flipped another page, hiding his amusement.

"Okay." Tom pulled out his wallet. "But I guarantee she'll wanna return it the second she opens it."

"Then you can blame me," Tara said as she went behind the counter and slipped the fabric off its fancy hanger. "But if she doesn't, I'm going to expect to see you in here again before her birthday. There's a bustier that she's been eyeing, too. That blue one there in the phone booth."

Tom looked vaguely horrified as he looked toward the phone booth. The satin and lacy thing hung inside as if a scantily clad, invisible woman was waiting there to make a telephone call. But he handed over a wad of cash and waited while Tara wielded tissue paper and a silver box.

"I can gift wrap it, if you like," she offered.

"I usually just give the stuff to her like it is."

Tara hesitated half a beat, her smile never wavering. "Okay." She started to slide the box into one of her fancy shopping bags.

Tom's increasingly harried gaze shifted to Axel.

"I'd go with the wrapping," Axel advised. Lord knew all the women in his family seemed to go gaga when something came in pretty paper and fancy ribbons.

"Mebbe you'd better wrap it," Tom told Tara hurriedly.

"Whatever you like." She slid the box out of the shopping bag. "I'll just be a moment." Taking it with her, she went into the back room.

"Good choice," Axel said in a low voice.

Tom made a face. He was practically whispering too, obviously hoping his comment wouldn't carry to the back room. "Janie's gonna think I've gone outta my tree bringing something home like that."

"She might be glad that you still think she's hot enough to wear something like that."

Tom's brow furrowed. "You think?"

Axel shrugged. "What do I know, man? You're the one who's been married fifteen years."

Tom suddenly looked like a lightbulb had gone off. "She *is* hot. Even in flannel." He shut up then as Tara glided back into the room, holding the fancy package aloft.

"What do you think?"

"It's real nice, Tara," Tom said hurriedly.

Tara beamed at him as she slid the gift into the shopping bag and added even more deftly folded pieces of shimmering white tissue. "Give it to her after a nice dinner. With candles. And no kids."

Tom's jaw dropped a little. "Er, yeah. Okay."

She handed over his change and the shopping bag.

Knowing when the getting was good, Tom grabbed both and hustled out of the door like the devil himself was at his heels.

The second the jingling door closed, Tara covered her mouth and giggled. Her eyes were dancing in a way that he hadn't seen in four long months. "That man has no idea what's in store for him," she said when her giggling finally stopped. "Janie Griffin has been in this shop every week oohing over that negligee set. But she was afraid to buy it herself, because she thinks Tom would laugh at her if she tried wearing something like that for him." She giggled again, shaking her head. "I see this sort of thing happen *all* the time."

"I take back what I said about you not being involved in the town anymore than you have to be," Axel said.

Her brows quirked. "Excuse me?"

"You're not just a shopkeeper." He eyed the lingerie corner. "You're probably responsible for keeping all the married folks around here from getting stuck in a rut."

"I don't know about that. But I do sell an amazing amount of it. Your mother—"

He held up his hand. "No. God, no. Please don't tell me about anything from that corner over there that my mother wears. Or that my father buys for her."

Tara's laughter filled the store. "Okay. I won't."

He pressed his face to the gleaming wood counter, but it was too late, because the notion was already there.

He lifted his head again as she went into the back room, still laughing.

It was also the first time he'd heard her laugh in four months. Truly laugh.

One way or another, he was going to make damn sure she never had a reason to stop.

## *Chapter Ten*

The next night, Tara sat propped in her bed and stared at the small article in the newspaper buried at the bottom of the "Nationally in Brief" page.

Trial Begins for Deuce's Cross Leaders

She'd read all ten sentences of the article about a hundred times since that morning when Axel had silently handed over the newspaper section, but she still read them again. As if she could glean something about Sloan from a total of seventy words.

Of course, there was no mention of her brother. Just the basics. That the long-awaited trial was finally beginning that day in Chicago.

Had Sloan been there? Was he safe? Would Axel at last unstick himself from her? Would she be able to go home to Chicago?

Did she even *want* to?

They were all questions that had churned behind her locked lips since Axel had given her the article and she'd told him, point-blank, that she didn't want to discuss it.

Her stomach rumbled despite the chamomile tea she'd been sipping. She set aside the newspaper and snapped off the bedside light. Turning on her side, she bunched the pillow into a more comfortable shape.

It was nearly midnight. She should be sleeping.

Instead, she was still lying there trying to will away the nausea that had dogged her all day. Crackers hadn't helped. Dry cereal that she'd snuck into her mouth when Axel wasn't looking hadn't helped. Tea hadn't helped.

Laying down *definitely* wasn't helping.

She sat up against the headboard and pressed her hands against the small swell of her abdomen. "Come on, baby," she whispered. "Give your mama a break."

But no break came. Her mind was too busy with fractured thoughts about Sloan, about Axel, about the baby. Finally, she shoved aside the covers and got up.

She silently opened her bedroom door and peered out into the hall. It was the fourth night Axel had slept on her couch. As usual, he made no sound as he slept. She padded to the other bedroom and closed the door before snapping on the task light above the larger of her two worktables.

If she wasn't going to sleep, then she might as well get *something* accomplished.

At least Axel wasn't distractingly glued to her hip.

Since that first day when he'd come to her, he hadn't left her even for an hour. She knew word about the two of them keeping constant company—even at her shop—was spreading around town, because the traffic in her store had easily doubled. As if the curious townspeople of Weaver wanted to see for themselves that Axel Clay was not only living in sin with the shopkeeper, but that he was so smitten he could even be found in her shop dusting shelves and running the register.

To her, Axel was a maddening distraction and not just because of the pregnancy she was keeping from him.

She slid out several trays of beads and stones and with no real plan in mind began arranging them on a specially grooved, felt-covered board. Eventually, the simple act of arranging and rearranging, of stringing and unstringing, managed to accomplish what bed and tea and crackers had not.

Her stomach stopped churning. Her head stopped pounding. Her thoughts stopped whirling.

Time slid by until she finished attaching one last clasp on a bracelet. She laid it next to the necklace and earrings. Each had been nothing but pieces in her supply trays when she'd first closed herself in the room. She'd take the jewelry to the shop the next morning—correction, later *that* morning—and price them there.

She left the worktable, tugged the sleeves of her oversized nightshirt back down her arms, and left the room as quietly as she'd entered. There were still a few good hours of sleep she could fit in.

But as she began crossing to her bedroom, a soft, unfamiliar sound made her stop cold.

Nothing but darkness was coming from the rest of the painfully silent house.

She cocked her head, listening harder while chills crept under her flesh.

Then she heard it again. More clearly. Her mind managed to identify the sound. Her plantation shutters were sliding open.

Was it Axel?

Or someone else?

She tried to swallow, but her mouth was suddenly too dry. She quietly stepped to the end of the hall and peeked around the corner. Axel's laptop was sitting open on the coffee table, emitting a faint, bluish glow. But it was enough to tell her that he wasn't sprawled on the couch—feet hanging over one end and arms over the other.

Instead, she could make out the shape of him standing near the front window.

"Stay there." His voice was almost soundless, and nearly startled her out of her skin.

How had he heard her?

The corner of the wall felt blessedly solid beneath her hand. "What's wrong?"

"There's a car out there that doesn't belong."

Her knees felt rubbery. "How—" She didn't bother voicing the rest of her question about how he could tell.

This was what he did, after all. Hadn't he told her that more than once?

She turned her back to the wall and slid down it until she was sitting on the floor. She wanted to tell him to get away from the window. Wanted to bury herself in her bed and pull the covers over her head, pretending that none of this was occurring.

Instead, she stayed right where she was, huddled in a ball with her head on her bent knees that she'd tucked under her nightshirt. And waited.

Just like she'd done so many times as a child.

She tried to close off the thoughts, the memories. Close off everything. But it was futile.

Then Axel said her name. His voice was soft, but not nearly the soundless whisper it had been before. "It's okay, Tara. You should go back to bed. It was Cynthia from across the street. Looks like she had a date. Everything's fine."

She lifted her head only to realize that he'd crouched down next to her. "All clear." Her voice was thin. "That's what my father used to say. It's *all clear.*"

Axel's hesitation was almost unnoticeable. "When did he say that?"

"Whenever it was safe again from whatever danger he figured we were in." After he'd sent her and Sloan and her mother into a huddled panic. "And then we'd have to leave. Move. My mother would grab the family photos and her mother's teapot. Sloan and I could only take what would fit into our backpacks. He'd take his favorite clothes."

Axel folded his hands around hers. "What did *you* take?"

She frowned a little. "Homework. From schools that I'd never go back to. Notes from the friends I'd managed to make who I'd never see again. Daddy would be annoyed, so my mom would always add as much of my clothes as she could to her suitcase. And my father—" she continued, but her throat felt knotted "—my father would get the briefcase."

"The briefcase?"

"Heavy. Black. Always locked and never unpacked. My mother told me once that it held all of our important stuff. Birth certificates. School records. Things like that." She'd dreaded seeing the briefcase come out, because it always meant more change.

She straightened her head again and looked at Axel. It was just as dark as ever, but her eyes had adjusted and she could make out the frown on his face and the faint gleam of his naked shoulders. "Sloan told me that he'd seen the briefcase open one time, and the only thing inside it was money."

"How often did you have to move?"

She lifted her shoulders slightly. "I don't know." That was a lie. "Thirty-seven times. All I ever wanted were roots somewhere." She heaved a sigh. "But I suppose my childhood is detailed in your logbook somewhere, too."

He exhaled. "Until you moved to Weaver, I didn't know a single thing about you. Hadn't heard of you or your brother." His hands tightened and he drew her to her feet. "Let's get you back to bed."

She went with him, feeling ridiculously docile. "You didn't know about my father?"

"No." He nudged her toward her four-poster, taking her robe from the mattress and tossing it over the back of the slipper chair in the corner.

Maybe she was the only one who heard the rattle of her prenatal vitamins still hidden in the robe's pocket.

"He was CIA," she said and felt defiant, even now, at saying the words aloud. But the rattle of those vitamins was rattling her even more. "To the rest of the world, he was a traveling salesman. But he wasn't selling anything. He was buying. Secrets. From all around the world. Doesn't that shock you?"

"No." He pulled back the covers and somehow, she obediently slid into bed. Then he snuggled the covers up, tucking her in like she was a baby.

She was acting like one, so why not?

Then he sat on the edge of the bed, his hip nudging against hers and she suddenly didn't feel infantile at all. Particularly when he was only wearing jeans and his shoulders stretched above her, broad and bare.

"It doesn't shock me. But I can see that it would be a hard life for a kid," he added.

She didn't want his sympathy or his understanding. Not when it made her conscience ache. "It's *no* life for a child."

"Probably not."

His sober agreement made her feel even worse and in the largest irony of all, she wanted more than anything for him to just lay down there beside her.

"It's that trial," she blurted out huskily.

He folded over the edge of her comforter. "You want to talk about it now?"

"No." She was painfully aware of his fingers on the comforter, so close to her breasts. "How, uh, how long do you think the trial will last?"

"They're predicting eleven weeks."

Dear Lord. Nearly three months.

She wouldn't be able to hide her pregnancy for one more month, much less three.

Nor could she seem to keep her hormones under control where Axel was concerned. His hip was burning through the layers of her blankets and cotton nightshirt right to her flesh. "I can't take three more months of this." It was true on every level.

"Why don't you close the shop tomorrow?"

She stared up at him. "And do what? Pretend that none of this is happening? The shop is all I have. I can't just close it on a whim."

"The shop isn't all you have. You've got me."

There was an ache deep inside her chest. "You're here because it's your *job*."

He didn't deny it. "Your shop is yours and you *can* do with it what you want."

About the only time in recent memory that she'd done what she wanted had been that stolen weekend in Braden with him.

And look what happened.

Her body…her heart…her life. They'd all been changed.

"If, for a day, you could go anywhere you wanted—do anything you wanted, what would it be?"

Frustration filled her. "I don't know."

"Come on, Tara. Use your imagination." His voice seemed to have dropped a notch.

Or maybe *that* was her imagination.

"Antiquing," she tossed out. "I can always find something for the shop when I go antiquing."

"That's work."

She exhaled. "Visit the bead shop down in Cheyenne, then! I don't know!"

"More work. Come on, Tara."

*Make love.*

It was all she could do to keep the words from escaping.

Her hand flopped, only to accidently brush against the satiny bulge of his bicep. Or maybe not-so-accidentally, considering. "What do you want me to say? And for the record, I *love* making jewelry. It's not just work to me."

"Okay then. We'll leave first thing in the morning."

His sudden capitulation threw her. "But—" She broke off. Because truly, what *would* be the harm in closing for just a day? "I can spend hours when I go there."

"Thanks for the warning. But we've got nothing but time."

She sank her head deeper into the pillow, peering at him. "Why are you being so agreeable?"

"Why are you being so suspicious? Changing your routine now and then is good for what ails you."

She nearly choked over that.

If he only knew.

"Will Mr. Hyde follow us down there, too?"

"Yes."

She absorbed his immediate response. At least he hadn't tried hiding it.

"So we'll leave in the morning." He pushed off the bed and for some reason, her mouth went dry as he stood, tall and broad, towering over her. "Everything will be okay, Tara. I promise you."

She couldn't manage a response to save her soul. So she just nodded. He must have seen, even in the dark. Or maybe he didn't, and it didn't matter.

Because he turned then and walked out of her room, closing the door quietly after him.

She stared after him, wide-eyed in the darkness, until she finally conquered the urge to call him back.

Only then did she finally hug the extra pillow against her and sleep.

* * *

"What are these things used for?" Axel held up a long, thin piece of metal.

Tara gave him an absent glance before looking back down at the tray of beads she was sorting through. "Making earrings." They'd been in the store for nearly two hours and it was pretty evident to her that Axel was bored out of his mind.

She wasn't going to let her conscience rush her, though. Not when she was so thoroughly enjoying poking and selecting and letting her creativity take the lead.

There were several chairs near one corner at the front of the shop, but Axel didn't go near them. The farthest he strayed from her was moving on the other side of the long display tables, covered from edge to edge with clear containers holding everything from tiny alphabet blocks to elegant cut stones and strikingly modern medallions.

He could *say* that the day was a little getaway, but his vigilance where she was concerned remained constant.

Oddly enough, though, she discovered that she didn't mind it so much. He wasn't hovering over her, looking menacingly at anyone who happened to brush too close. He was just… there.

"Stevie Stuart, you stop running this very instant." The woman's harried voice wasn't quite enough to prepare Tara for the dark-haired bullet that shot past her out of nowhere and she hastily lifted her tray out of the way.

"Sorry." A young woman, heavily pregnant and looking apologetic, huffed along the path burned by the little speed demon. "I should have known he'd go wild if I brought him here."

"Hold on there, buddy." Axel caught the young boy by the back of his shirt as he sped past him. "Where's the fire?"

The little boy stared up at Axel, abruptly fascinated. "There's a fire?"

"There *is* no fire, Stevie, except the one burning under your feet." The boy's mother waddled around the table to grab her son's hand and drew him away, muttering to him in hushed tones.

Axel was grinning as he watched them go. "Cute kid."

Tara opened her mouth, only to realize what was on the tip of her tongue. "Yes," she agreed hurriedly and knelt down to pick up the items that had fallen out of her tray before she could make the monumental mistake of telling him about the baby. Right there in the middle of the Bead Me Up store.

"Here." Axel crouched next to her and handed her a medallion that had rolled under the table.

She couldn't look at him. She took the medallion and dropped it in the tray, then pushed to her feet, brushing her hands down the sides of her slacks. "I'm done."

He straightened, too. "Great. In time for something to eat."

She couldn't help her start of surprise. "We had lunch two hours ago." They'd stopped at a café when they'd arrived in Cheyenne.

"So?"

She shook her head a little and drew out her wallet as the salesclerk tallied up her selections. Axel handed her coat to her and took the bag when the clerk finished, and with Axel's hand on the small of her back, they returned to his truck and he drove to a nearby ice cream parlor.

"You're like a kid in a candy store," she murmured when she followed him inside and he deliberated the choices.

"There are two dozen flavors. If you order vanilla, I might have to turn you over my knee."

"I wasn't going to order vanilla," she lied.

He laughed softly and brushed his finger down her nose. "Freckles are showing."

Her face went even hotter. "I don't want ice cream, anyway."

He cocked his head slightly toward her. "Would you prefer chocolate cake?"

Her mouth ran dry. Axel in protector mode was something she was becoming accustomed to. Axel in any other mode was too dangerous for words.

"Um, sorry sir, but we don't have chocolate cake here." The acne-dotted teenager standing at the counter looked confused. "The list of flavors is up there." He gestured with his ice cream scoop at the menu hanging above his head.

Axel slanted another look her way. "What do you think, Tara?"

She gave him the sternest look she could muster. "Chocolate cake isn't on the menu."

"That doesn't mean I don't want it."

And then, leaving her quaking, he grinned at the boy behind the counter. "Two cones, please. Vanilla."

## *Chapter Eleven*

"How old do you suppose that kid was?" They were back on the highway leaving town, vanilla ice cream cones eaten. "Stevie Stuart. The miniature, human cannonball."

Tara looked from the side-view mirror where she could see Mason Hyde's ramshackle truck several car lengths behind them. "I don't know. Five? Six? Why?"

"No reason." He flipped a heater vent toward her. "You warm enough?"

"Yes." She was more than warm enough. Her taste buds were still satiated by vanilla ice cream. But the rest of her was hung up on…chocolate cake.

"You ever think about having kids?"

She closed her eyes, dying. "I'm thirty years old." It was the best she could manage.

His thumb tapped the steering wheel. "Biological clock ticking?"

Her tongue felt the size of Alaska. "Something like that." She hesitated for several thick beats. "You?"

"Some day." His voice was careless as he picked up speed to pass a slower-moving trailer. "You might have noticed the Clays are big on family."

"Yes." She spotted Mason's truck again. This time about five vehicles back. "How did you, um, get into the body-guarding business?"

"The agency doesn't do only personal security."

She didn't want to be curious but she was. "What else does it—*you*—do?"

"Make the world a safer place. That's the reason why the agency exists, anyway." His lips twisted a little. "I don't know how well I've fit into that picture."

"Why?"

He just shook his head, and she thought he wasn't going to answer. But after a long moment, he did. "I've failed at the most important thing I could have done."

She turned a little toward him. "What?" Then she frowned. "Or can't you say?" That had been her father's typical refrain when she'd want to know why they had to uproot their lives again.

"Yeah." His voice was gruff. "I can't say."

She eyed his profile. The weight he seemed to feel was like a tangible thing, and she wished she hadn't brought it up. "I'm sure you'd change things, if you could."

His gaze slanted toward her. "Do you believe that?"

She suddenly felt out of her depth, and wasn't entirely certain why. "Yes." She hesitated. "I…I think you take your professional responsibilities very seriously."

He looked back at the road. His thumb stopped tapping the wheel. "And my personal ones?"

She opened her mouth. But it was a while before she could even form words. "I…I don't know you well enough to say."

He snorted softly. "Right. We didn't get to know each other at *all* that weekend."

She straightened in her seat, feeling scorched. "I don't know how you ended up doing the work that you do." She pressed her hands together. "You come from a town that's hardly a dot on the map. Where's the leap from that, to this Hollins-Winword stuff?" Her father had been recruited into *his* service just after graduating from Yale.

"Family connections." His voice was dry.

His family were primarily ranchers with a few lawmen and businessmen tossed in. She found it difficult drawing a line from that to what Axel did for a living. It was her turn to sound disbelieving. "Right."

He just shrugged, though, not choosing to elaborate.

She plucked at the hem of the long sweater she was wearing. "Do you ever think you'd get out of it?" She moistened her lips, feeling terribly careful. "Do the horse-breeding thing full-time?"

But he didn't answer. He just switched lanes again. "Are you going to go back to writing for magazines again?"

"After Sloan's case is resolved?" She turned her palms upward for a moment. "I don't know."

His thumb silently tapped the steering wheel. "Do you miss it?"

"Yes," she answered promptly.

He slanted her a look. "What do you miss about it?"

"I—" she said and then broke off. What *did* she miss about working at the magazine? "The creativity of it."

He smiled. "Seems like you're showing plenty of that with all the jewelry you make."

"It's not the same."

"How so?"

She started to give him an answer only to realize she didn't have one. Had she ever spent a sleepless night working on an article so she could relax enough to go back to sleep?

She honestly couldn't remember.

"There was nothing in the paper this morning about the trial." Not that she'd really expected there to be.

"No." He adjusted his rearview mirror. Switched lanes again.

She finally noticed the speedometer and looked out at the mirror on her door. Mason's truck was closer again. Three cars behind. "Are you in a hurry to get back to Weaver?"

"No."

She tilted her head, giving the speedometer another glance. "Then why are you going nearly thirty over the speed limit?"

"Because I want to shake the truck that's been following us for the past twenty miles."

"Mason Hyde's been following us in his truck."

"Mason's in a Corvette today."

She went stiff and turned to look out the back window. "I haven't seen a Corvette." Only that ramshackle truck that she'd believed was the same one Mason drove.

"That's because Mason is good at what he does. Turn around."

She turned around to face the front. Alarm had her heart suddenly ready to climb up her throat. "You're going to get stopped for speeding."

"Maybe." He pulled around a semi and went even faster. Without taking his eyes from the road, he pulled out his cell phone and hit a few buttons, then lifted it to his ear. "Mason. You get the license on that truck called in?" He listened for a moment. "Keep trying." He disconnected and dropped the phone on the console between their seats. "It's going to be fine, Tara."

She pushed her hair behind her ears. "Sure. Fine." Her voice was shaky. She pressed her palm to her belly, carefully pulling in a deep breath. Letting it out just as slowly. *Everything's fine. Just fine.*

Axel's phone beeped and she nearly jumped out of her skin.

He lifted the phone to his ear again. "Yeah."

Almost immediately, the speedometer's needle dropped away from the red zone where it had been nearly buried.

Tara's breath rushed out of her and she leaned her head against the headrest, feeling weak.

"Thanks, Mason." Axel set the phone again on the console. "Truck just took a turnoff."

Her heartbeat began settling down, though it still left her feeling queasy.

The same way she'd always felt after one of her father's alerts. "Nobody cares that I'm Sloan McCray's sister, Axel. Nobody."

"I care."

She pressed her lips together. "That's not what I meant."

He gave her a quick glance. "I know. And maybe we are all being paranoid. But I'd rather be cautious than take a chance with you."

Everything inside her squeezed. "Because Sloan hired you," she pointed out. Reminding her silly, silly heart.

"That's one reason."

"What other reasons would there be?"

He looked at her. His eyes seemed more gold than brown. "You know why."

She swallowed. Hard. "You don't have to feel responsible just because we once…once slept together."

"As I recall, it was more than *once…once.* Several times more than *once…once.*"

A flush burned from her head to the toes she was curling inside her low-heeled boots. "One weekend," she allowed, sounding mortifyingly prim.

"Best damn weekend of my life," he murmured.

"Right," she countered. She couldn't prevent the scoff. "That's why you snuck out while I was sleeping."

"I tried to wake you. But you were dead to the world."

"I'd had too much to drink."

He snorted softly. “The only drinks you had were in the Suds-n-Grill the first night. You’d had too many orgasms.”

She looked out the window, feeling scorched. “In your dreams,” she lied.

His hand caught hers, and wouldn’t release her even when she yanked. “Every night,” he said, his voice flat, “every night since then I’ve thought about you. About us.”

“There *is* no *us,* Axel.” She couldn’t afford for there to be. Unfortunately, she wasn’t sure just who she was reminding more. Him, or her. “There’s one weekend that was a fluke, and then there is the paycheck you earn to watch me. That’s not an us.”

“What if I wasn’t earning that paycheck?”

“Men like you never give up that sort of career.” He had even avoided answering that very issue not ten minutes earlier.

“Men like me. What the hell is that supposed to mean?”

“Men like *you!*” Her voice rose and she struggled to bring it back down. “Like Sloan. Like my father. You live two lives and it works perfectly well for you, but for—” She started but then broke off again.

“But for the rest of you, it takes its toll,” he concluded.

She refused to acknowledge the stinging deep behind her eyes. “Yes. The rest of us get to pay the price.”

He was silent for a long while. “I’m sorry.”

She stared ahead while the snowy countryside whizzed past their windows. “So am I.”

“For what it’s worth,” he said after a long while, “not every family involved with this sort of work is like yours was.”

She just shook her head. “You don’t know that.”

“Yeah. I do.” He waited a beat. “Family connections, remember?”

She laughed, disbelieving. “Okay, so you have some distant uncle somewhere who introduced you to someone, who introduced you to someone, and so on and so forth.”

He suddenly veered toward the shoulder of the road, pulling right off the highway.

"What are you doing?" She grabbed the armrest as they rocked to a stop. Over his shoulder, she saw a black Corvette fly past them. But Mason didn't pull off near them. He just kept driving.

Axel turned in his seat toward her, evidently unconcerned with Mason. "It is an uncle. And he's not distant. It's a lot of people, actually. And they're not distant, either."

She pressed her hand to the nerves jangling in her belly. "What are you trying to say?"

"I'm saying that I *know* not all families are like yours, because I know what *my* family is like."

"Your father raises horses. Practically everyone in the state knows that."

"Yeah. But he didn't always. Hollins-Winword doesn't possess anything as typical as an office complex, but if they did, there'd be a wall of greats and my father would be smack-dab in the middle of it. He ran more black ops in his time there than any other agent, before or since. But he was smart enough to recognize when it was time to get out."

She tried to reconcile the man she knew with the one Axel described, and failed. "And when was that?"

"When he married my mother."

"So you don't know. He was *out* when you were growing up. You have roots, Axel. The kind that Sloan and I never even had an opportunity to sprout!"

"You're missing my point, Tara. My father wasn't—isn't—the only one in the business. And they've all raised families. Normal families. They didn't move around every six months. They didn't keep all of their worldly possessions tucked into a backpack. Not everyone involved in this sort of work lives a life like you experienced."

She didn't want to believe him. Because if she did, then

what sort of person did that make her for continuing to keep quiet about her pregnancy?

She, who hated secrets, was keeping the biggest one of all. "None of this matters anyway," she said, looking blindly out the window because it was so much easier than facing those golden-brown eyes of his. "I had a life in Chicago. Once Sloan's case is over—" She bit her lip.

"You'll go back. To a house you don't own anymore. To a magazine you don't write for."

The words were only the truth.

A truth that plagued her.

She adjusted the seat belt resting over her lap, so very near the tiny life growing inside her. "Why would I stay in Weaver?"

She heard him exhale and he abruptly set the truck back into motion. "Good damn question," he muttered.

And then, they said no more.

For the rest of that week, Axel didn't suggest again that she close the shop, though he seemed to find plenty of things for them to do before going home at the end of the workday. Stopping by his brother-in-law's clinic to discuss some horse he wanted to buy. Driving around town with the excuse that he just wanted to see what changes had occurred while he'd been gone.

She'd quickly learned there was no point in arguing. After a day at the shop, she wanted nothing more than to go home. Yet it was so apparent that he was avoiding being alone with her any more than necessary.

In the morning, after showering and dressing for work, she'd find a cup of herbal tea waiting for her in the kitchen while he took his crack at the shower. At the shop, he moved displays and unpacked boxes and even—when she had to take a quick break for the ladies' room—rang up a sale to Tom Griffin just before closing on Saturday. The man, flush with success over his anniversary gift, ran in to purchase the bustier hanging in the phone booth.

The only thing Tara needed to do when she returned to the front of the shop was tuck a few more sheets of pearlescent tissue inside the bag that Axel was ready to hand over to Tom.

The man was practically skipping when he darted out of the store, and Tara couldn't help but smile a little as she turned around the Closed sign and locked the door.

Axel looked as amused as she felt when her gaze landed on him.

But the relative silence that had lasted for days between them reared its ugly head. She turned away to straighten the folds in a handmade quilt hanging over an iron rod near the front window. "I, um, I need to stop at the grocery store sometime soon. We're out of milk."

"We'll go on the way home." His lips quirked. "We sound like some old, comfortable couple."

She stopped fiddling with the quilt's already-perfect folds. "Only you're not old."

"Neither are you."

They also weren't a couple, but she knew there was no point in pointing out the obvious.

She moved behind the register, pulled out the cash drawer and gathered up the sales receipts for the day. Then she carried them into the back to lock in the safe, while Axel turned out the lights in the front of the shop.

With him around, there was no need for her to do any of her usual after-hours tasks that she typically did when the store was closed. Because he was taking care of most of them while she was open.

That left more hours of the day back at her place that had to be filled with something. The only positive result was that she'd made a serious dent in replacing much of the jewelry that she'd sold at the Valentine's Festival.

She spun the lock on the safe and turned out the lights in the back, then waited until Axel gave that abbreviated "all's clear" honk from his vehicle before slipping out the rear door and straight into the truck.

He had his cell phone at his ear. "See you then," he said, and hung up. "My mom," he told Tara as he put the truck in gear and drove out of the narrow alleyway. "Wants us to come by for dinner."

"Aren't we going to go there tomorrow for Sunday dinner?" Axel had already told her that they would be.

"Yeah, but this'll just be us."

She bit back her protest, knowing it would be futile, anyway. "I still need to get some milk."

"Don't worry. You won't miss out on your calcium."

She tightened her seat belt and shushed her conscience for about the millionth time. When he turned the opposite direction of her house, though, she realized he intended to drive out to his parents' place right then and there. "Can't we go home first so I can change?"

She couldn't stop the pinpricks of awareness that sprung up from the gaze he slid over her. "You look fine."

She dashed her hand down the front of her beige ankle-length skirt. It was one of the few items in her closet that still fit.

Pretty soon, she was going to have to go shopping for different clothes.

Maternity clothes.

She chewed the inside of her lip as they drove out of town. As had become her habit, she kept watch in the rearview mirror for any sign of Mason Hyde following them in one of his apparently ever-changing fleet of vehicles.

If she hadn't met him that first day at the shop and seen him speeding past them when she and Axel were on their way back from Cheyenne, she wouldn't know the man existed.

One of Axel's nearly invisible "guardian angels."

"Will your sister and her family be there?"

"No. They went to Braden for the night."

Tara couldn't afford to think too long about Braden.

"I suppose your parents know what you really do for a living."

"Yes."

"Then why keep up the pretense for them where we… where we're concerned?"

"What conclusions they draw are theirs."

"I don't understand that kind of thinking. Not when they know what you do."

"You really want to know why I don't talk about you with them? Because they'll see right through me just like they always have. They'll know I'm—" he said, then broke off, exhaling sharply. "They'll know you're *not* just an assignment."

Her lips parted.

"They'll know I *am* interested in you. So you see, it really doesn't matter whether I tell them about this assignment or not. And I can assure you that, of any secrets I'm keeping, *this* one is the least of my worries!" He gave her a glance that was searing. "Are you satisfied now?"

She slowly closed her mouth.

He gave one sharp nod, and they finished the drive in silence.

## *Chapter Twelve*

"Thank you for dinner," Tara told Emily several hours later. "It was delicious."

Axel's mother beamed. "Honey, you can come any time you like. Particularly since it's one way of getting Axel to show his face around here." She reached up to kiss her son's cheek. "You'll be here tomorrow, too. Right? We're going to have a cake for Justin's twenty-first birthday."

Axel grimaced. "He's too young to be turning twenty-one already."

"That's what we say about all of you." Emily sent Tara an impish smile. "When you have kids of your own, you'll see."

"God help us," Axel deadpanned. He lifted his head toward his father, who was looking at some vacation snapshots that Rebecca and Sawyer had brought with them.

They'd arrived just minutes before Axel started herding Tara toward the door.

Tara barely had a chance to say anything before Axel nudged

her out and she had to practically skip to keep up with him as they headed to his pickup. "What's the sudden rush to get back to town?"

He pulled open the passenger door for her. "I'm not in a hurry to go back to Weaver." He tucked the hem of her coat inside before closing her door and going around to his side. "I want to go by my cabin," he told her as he started the engine. "Won't take long."

She'd longed to see his cabin since he'd described it to her in Braden, but she shrugged as if she didn't care one way or the other.

He'd told her the cabin wasn't far from his parents' house, but it was certainly far enough. The road leading there wasn't even paved and before long, even the lights from the outbuildings were out of sight. "How can you tell where you're going?" The night was black as pitch, his headlights reflecting back the sheen of snow.

"I grew up here. There's not a foot of land around this place that I don't know like the back of my hand." He went around another curve then pulled to a stop.

"Watch your step," he said when he came around to open her door. "The snow's deep."

Sure enough, her black boots sank at least four inches as they waded toward the shadowy door of the darkened structure. But when they went up several steps to a wide porch, even in the dark, she found it alarmingly easy to imagine old-fashioned rocking chairs, great pots of blooming flowers and icy pitchers of lemonade.

She blinked hard, but the appealing image didn't fade.

He unlocked the door. "Come on in."

She followed him inside where he flipped on switches as he went, flooding the interior with golden light. The entry turned toward the right and opened into an unexpectedly large room.

Thoughts of rocking on a warm summer day on the front

porch were small potatoes in comparison to the pleasure that sank right into her bones at the sight before her.

Rough-hewn logs formed the exterior walls that were studded with sky-high windows. The interior walls were a smooth off-white color devoid entirely of decoration—a canvas just waiting for the right touches. Natural wood planks covered the floor.

Other than an enormous, stone-fronted fireplace, there was a large pool table situated almost directly opposite where she stood, a half-dozen large packing crates, and the couch he'd bought from her shop.

"What do you think?"

She loved it. All of it. "The couch looks good," she admitted. The day after he'd bought it, several of his cousins had hauled the massive couch away in a truck with the Double-C logo printed on the door. Now, she looked at the piece, perfectly situated in front of the fireplace.

Her overactive imagination had no trouble at all imagining the two of them sharing its enveloping space while a fire roared in front of them.

*You and I are going to make love on that couch.*

She quickly looked away from the couch, but the memory of his words still echoed in her head.

"I like it." He stood in the center of the room, hands on his hips, looking around. "Rest of the cabin is still pretty empty, though. Walls are too bare."

Personally, she thought "cabin" was far too modest a word. "What else do you need?" She wandered over to the pool table. Even it was a masterpiece with its gleaming dark wood and weighty, carved legs. There was a pendant light hanging over the center of the deep green felt, but she imagined that he rarely had to use the artificial light during the day, since the table was situated in front of three floor-to-ceiling windows that were angled to take in the sunlight.

"Why? You want to add some more sales to your coffers?"

She couldn't help but smile at that. "Once a shopkeeper, always a shopkeeper."

"I need a king-size headboard for my bed."

She swallowed a little. "I'll keep an eye out for one." There was an open carton sitting on the floor near the base of one of the windows and she knelt next to it, plucking out one of the photo frames stacked inside.

Axel, flanked by his beaming parents and wearing his college cap and gown, sent a wicked grin up at her from the picture.

Her fingers walked through the rest of the frames, getting a glance at nearly a dozen shots chronicling the Clay family. "Here's some of the answer to your bare walls. Hang these up." She held one of the frames for him to see. "They have similar frames. They'd look wonderful hanging together."

"Maybe if someone with an eye for that sort of thing hung them." His voice was leading.

She sent him a skeptical look. "Don't try to convince me that your mother or your sister or your cousins haven't already offered to help."

"Are you kidding? They'd swarm the place if I let them." He looked appalled at the very idea of it.

"But they have excellent taste."

"It'd be their taste."

"But you want me to do it."

"I don't mind having *your* taste."

Everything inside her liquefied.

And from the look in his eyes, she knew he was perfectly aware of the way his words had sounded.

She swallowed against the heartbeat threatening to choke her and grabbed the carton as she rose. She placed it on the pool table and began unloading the frames, spreading them out on the dark green felt.

After a moment, she felt more than heard his sigh as he

came up next to her, planting his hands wide on the side of the pool table. "What are you doing?"

"Seeing what sort of arrangement might look best." She was going to act as if she weren't ready to dissolve from need if it killed her. "Who's the guy in the navy whites?" She picked up the informal shot of Axel and several other men, most of whom she recognized, standing with their beer mugs held aloft.

"Ryan. My cousin. Rebecca and Sawyer's oldest."

She set the frame back into the arrangement. She'd never met Ryan Clay, but had certainly heard about his death. For one thing, he was the son of the retired sheriff and the most prominent doctor in town. For another, he'd been a serviceman. The entire town had nearly shut down the day his memorial service had been held. But the small black-and-white memorial photo of an unsmiling soldier that had been carried in the local paper barely resembled the carefree-looking guy in Axel's photograph. "Were you close?"

"Yeah." His voice was as gruff as hers was soft. "He's—he was a few years older than me, but we were best friends, pretty much."

She looked up at him and the hard set of his jaw. The dark shadows filling his eyes.

Before she knew what she was doing, she'd rested her fingers on top of his broad hand. "I'm sorry." She hadn't lost Sloan to death—she'd prayed every night that she never would. But she still felt as if he were lost to her, anyway. "It must be very painful."

He turned his hand and caught her fingers. "I'd rather talk about nearly anything else."

She moistened her lips. "H-how about whether you have a hammer and nails?"

His eyes burned over her face for a long moment. "Okay. Coming up."

She tucked her tingling fingers into a fist when he left the room, and looked back at the photographs. But she wasn't really seeing them.

He was back too quickly for her to master the emotion swirling around inside her.

"Nails." He set a small box on the felt. "Hammer." He held it up. "Point me where you want me."

She tucked her tongue behind her teeth for a moment. When she was certain "the couch" wouldn't escape, she picked up the largest frame from the pool table and carried it to the wall adjacent the front door. She held up the photo of his mother and father on their wedding day, envisioning its placement as the center of the arrangement. "Nail there."

"Looks a little low to me."

"I thought you trusted me."

His lips twisted a little, but he deftly set the nail.

"Do you have a pencil and a level?"

"I wasn't a Boy Scout—" he said as he pulled both out of his back pocket "—but I can be prepared."

She quickly turned to face the wall, using the level to mark the rest of the nail placements.

He'd been prepared the night in Braden, and she'd gotten pregnant, anyway.

Proof positive that the ninety-nine-percent-effective statement on the little box of condoms they'd bought at the same store as the birthday cake really didn't mean one-hundred-percent foolproof.

"Real picture hangers would be better than nails," she murmured. "I don't suppose—"

"No. We'll bring some the next time we come out here, and you can change out the nails for 'em," he said.

Next time? There was going to be a next time?

She shouldn't feel the least bit excited about that prospect, but a curl of something dangerous twined through her anyway.

What she needed to be doing was keeping a distance between herself and Axel because once he'd moved on from being her bodyguard, that would be that.

He could say a family could be "normal" given the kind of work he did. But she'd lived too long knowing otherwise.

She finished making her pencil marks and after Axel set the nails, she finished hanging the frames.

"Looks good to me," he said when she stepped back to study them.

"Not quite yet." She switched two frames.

"You didn't warn me we'd be playing musical picture frames."

"You said you weren't in any hurry to get back to Weaver." She took the empty box and put it on the pool table. "But I'm done, anyway. So what do you think?"

His hand slid up her spine. Slowly settled on her nape. "I think it's time we stopped pretending."

Tara went still. She closed her eyes. Her fingers tightened over the edge of the pool table. "Axel—"

His thumb stroked along the side of her neck.

She trembled and hauled in a deep breath. Exhaled on his name. Weak. That's what she was. "Axel. I want…I mean I don't want—"

"Sh." His lips hovered around her car. All down the back of her she could feel the heat of him penetrating the thick knit of her sweater, the thin fabric of her skirt. "I'll tell you what *I* want." His other hand slid around her waist from behind, his palm flattening over her abdomen.

She sucked in another breath, redolent with desire…and alarm.

Where was her head?

She shouldn't be allowing him to touch her. Shouldn't be contemplating making love with him.

"What I've wanted for days." His voice lowered even more,

until it rumbled, deep and low across her nerve endings. "What I've thought about for weeks. Months. No matter how hard I try not to."

"Axel—"

"I want to touch you." His words burned against her ear almost as hotly as did his hand as it slowly began inching downward. "Taste you." His teeth caught her earlobe in a gentle, seductive tug. "Again."

She bit the inside of her lip, hard, when his fingers grazed the juncture of her thighs, right through her skirt. "Axel—"

"I want to hear my name on your lips when I slide into you. Hear you make that little gasp you make when I slide—" while his hand delved further, taking the fabric with it "—almost out again."

Heat steamed through her veins. She frantically grabbed his hand, but couldn't make herself pull him away. "Is this why you brought me here?"

"Are you going to be mad if I said yes?"

She trembled. "I don't know."

"I wanted you to see my place." His voice dropped even lower. "I wanted to see you *in* my place."

Her heart squeezed. "We really shouldn't." Her voice was faint. More like a plea to be convinced otherwise, than the stand every logical cell she possessed knew she should be taking.

"You're right. I'd be yanked from this detail in a heartbeat if it got out that I'd crossed this line again. But I can't make myself care right now about the *shouldn'ts.* So there's only one question left." His hand intimately glided again. Cupped between her legs. His other hand settled against the underside of her breast, his thumb unerringly finding the hard point of her nipple even through her thick sweater. "Do you really want me to stop?"

Did she want to stop the madness?

Or did she want to sink into it, into him, without any regard for the consequences?

His hand moved against her again and her ability for decision-making slid right out of her, alongside her dissolving knees.

Her head fell back weakly against his chest. "No." The admission was oddly freeing. "Don't stop."

He let out a low, harsh breath then and spun her around to face him. His mouth covered hers.

The earth seemed to fall away as their tongues tangled.

He tasted of coffee. And deep, dark bliss.

And then she felt the side rail of the pool table beneath her and realized he'd lifted her up onto it. He nudged her legs apart and stepped between them. His hands gathered folds of her skirt as he ran them up to her knees. Her thighs.

Her arms slid around his shoulders, grasping for steadiness. And when she felt his fingers slide against her hips, fingertips looping over the sides of her stretchy lace panties to draw them down, she was pathetically eager to help.

They were all the way down to her knees when she realized her boots would get in the way. "My boots—"

But he solved the matter by simply giving the lacy panties one swift tug. They tore and he tossed them aside.

Her breath rushed through her, oddly intoxicated.

And then his fingers grazed her.

There.

She hissed out a breath, her fingers closing around his shoulders. Sliding through his hair. "Axel—"

"That's the sound." His voice was low. Fierce. His fingers delved. Slid. Tormented. His mouth burned over hers. "Tell me you want this as much as I do."

"I want this as much as you do," she whispered. Then she couldn't say another word, because everything inside her was suddenly bursting out of control. And all she could do was gasp and shudder and cling as he drove her right off the precipice, and she was still quaking when he worked his belt loose and pulled her hard, right onto himself.

She cried out, clutching his shoulders, feeling so perfectly impaled by him that she shot up toward that peak again without ever having hit bottom.

His breath was harsh against her ear as he carried her to the couch, never parting from her. "We're going to take more time next time," he said, following her down onto the leather.

She couldn't fathom a next time, because she couldn't fathom surviving the endless pleasure careening through her. Her mouth found his, her legs twining around his.

Skirt and jeans tangled, but it didn't matter.

Nothing mattered but him.

And just when she thought she couldn't bear the sensation coiling inside her another moment without screaming from it, he tensed, bracing his hand on the leather above her head, and muttered her name.

She splintered, everything inside her greedily, keenly clutching as she felt the pulse of him in the very heart of her.

Only when the world started spinning again did he lower his head until it hit her shoulder. "This is a good couch," he muttered.

Her lips curved. A weak laugh escaped.

And then he moved, sliding off her and the couch and she had to tamp down hard on the protest that rose to her lips. Quick and needful.

He raked his fingers through his hair and turned toward her. "Tara—"

"Yo, yo, yo." The loud deep voice hailed them just as the front door creaked open and heavy boots sounded on the wood floor.

## *Chapter Thirteen*

Tara stiffened like a branding iron had pressed against her spine at the sound of people just minutes away from discovering them.

She frantically rolled off the couch, nearly tripping over her long skirt, and darted into the kitchen with no real thought other than escape.

Mercifully, there was a small powder room off the kitchen and she slammed the door shut, pressing back against the wood while her heart hammered inside her ears almost—but not quite—loudly enough to block out the voices she could hear from the other room.

Shaking, she splashed water over her face, and pulled the small beige towel off the ring next to the pedestal sink, pressing it to her forehead. Her flushed cheeks.

Maybe whoever it was would leave. Quickly.

But no sooner than she formed that hopeful thought, she

heard the voices grow louder. Heavy boots sounded on the wood floor. They were in the kitchen.

Cringing, she held her breath until the voices receded again.

She stared at herself in the narrow mirror above the sink. This is what she got for doing something she shouldn't have done.

Particularly with the secret she was holding.

She resolutely squared her shoulders and finished freshening up, but her resolution quailed when she realized she'd altogether forgotten her panties out in the living area.

Where had they left them?

On the pool table?

The floor?

She exhaled shakily and yanked open the door, her skirt swishing around the ankles of her boots as she walked through the empty kitchen with—please, please—no one the wiser that she was thoroughly bare beneath.

The voices, she learned quickly enough, belonged to Axel's cousins, Casey and Erik.

"They came to shoot some pool," Axel told her when she reappeared, her gaze furtively searching the floor for a distinctive hank of lace.

"Didn't figure you'd even be here what with all the time you've spent at Tara's," Erik said. He held a longneck bottle toward her. "Want one?"

"No thanks." She smiled, but it felt stiff.

She'd spotted her panties.

Barely hidden beneath the toe of Axel's boots.

"I told 'em we were heading back to town." Axel's voice showed none of the strain hers did.

"Yes. Right." She willed her face not to flush, but it was a futile effort at best. She felt like a teenager caught necking.

Only she'd never been a teenager who'd necked.

"That's cool." Erik selected a pool cue from the rack that had yet to be hung on the wall. "We're still gonna shoot, though."

"Not all of us are *love*birds," Casey added, grinning.

Tara quickly moved away from the pool table. She had a smile on her face, she was certain of it, because her lips felt as if they were sticking to her teeth.

"Go ahead and give me grief," Axel drawled. "The two of you hanging out here on a Saturday night, shooting pool with only each other's mug to look at? Really sad."

Casey grunted. "That's pretty low."

Erik grunted, too. "And pretty damn true." He twisted the top off his bottle to take a healthy swig. "Could drive a guy to drink."

Axel bent down and picked up one of the bottles from the cardboard carrier sitting on the floor.

If she weren't so mortified, Tara would probably have been impressed with the imperceptible way he managed to tuck away her ruined panties in his jeans' pocket beneath his loose shirttails all at the same time, with neither of his cousins the wiser.

"Yeah. Root beer." He set the bottle of old-fashioned root beer on the rail and shook his head again. "If you're going to mope around because you can't get a girl, at least be a man about it and drink real beer."

"I like root beer," Erik defended.

Casey slid another cue out of the rack and rolled it against the felt. "And I like not having to pay for pool like we do at Colby's."

"You don't have to pay for pool at Colby's."

"We do now," he groused. "You haven't been there in a month of Sundays, Ax, so you don't know. New owner's rules. And since you're never here anyway…" He shrugged again, leaving the rest unsaid.

"I thought both of your parents had pool tables at their homes." Tara distinctly remembered talk about that around the dinner table at the big house.

"They do." Axel had a glint in his eyes that she wasn't sure was owed to their near discovery or not. "But neither one of them want to play at their folks' places because their dads will want to play, too, and they'll mop the floor with them."

Casey grimaced. "Also sad, but true."

"My dad and uncles can whip almost anyone around here when it comes to pool," Axel explained.

"And poker," Casey added.

"And drinking." Erik tilted his bottle to his lips. "The real stuff," he said after he lowered it again.

Tara tried to envision the men she knew with the picture their sons were painting and found it difficult. Just as difficult as it was to see any of them involved in the kind of work that Axel had described. The Clay family in general was about the most responsible, upstanding, salt-of-the-earth kind of people she'd ever met.

"Oh." Hardly a stellar response. But then she was standing there clutching her hands together as if they contained all of her lost marbles while cool air drifted maddeningly up her long skirt in a needless reminder that her panties were residing in Axel's front pocket. "Maybe we should be going," she suggested.

Axel's arm slid around her stiff shoulders. "Good idea, sweetheart." He directed her toward the door. "Turn off the lights when you guys leave."

"Always do." Casey and Erik had already lost interest and were racking up the balls on the table.

Axel grabbed their coats from the coatrack by the door and Tara rapidly shoved her arms in the sleeves when he held hers for her. As soon as he let go, she yanked open the heavy door and hurried outside.

The night air slapped her burning cheeks with a welcome chill as she strode to his truck. Inside, she snapped on her safety belt, keeping her eyes resolutely ahead even when Axel got behind the wheel and she could feel the weight of his gaze on her.

After a moment, he started the engine and backed away from the cabin and the other pickup parked there. "It could have been a lot worse," he pointed out. "They could have walked in ten minutes earlier."

Her thighs clenched. Hard. "This doesn't change anything. We…we're not doing this again. You're still not sharing my bed when we get home."

"Some men might take words like that as a challenge," Axel remarked. He turned the headlights to high. "Fortunately, I'm not one of them."

"Good, because the moment has *definitely* passed." She stared out the side window. What a liar she was, sitting there, her body shockingly tight with tension and still shockingly wet with want. "I don't know what we were thinking."

"I know what I was thinking." His voice was like gravel, but after that he blessedly said no more.

They passed the lights of his parents' house and soon they'd reached the highway.

They'd been driving for nearly a half hour and Axel could practically feel the freeze warning exuding from Tara's pores. "I'm not going to apologize," he warned.

He'd be damned if he would.

Whether or not he knew better than to cross that line with her while assigned to protect her, *she'd* wanted him just as badly as he'd wanted her. And he wanted her still, all over again. He was beginning to think he always would.

"I didn't ask for an apology." Her voice was cool.

"Good." He ignored the caveman urge to kiss that cool tone right out of her. But it wasn't easy.

They rounded the last sweeping curve before Weaver when his phone beeped, and he snatched it up. "Yeah."

Max Scalise's voice greeted him, fully in lawman mode.

And it had every hair on Axel's body standing on end.

"I'll be there as soon as I can," he said and slammed the phone back on the console.

Tara's face was a pale blur. "What's wrong?"

"There's a fire." He hesitated. "At your house."

She jerked. "What?"

But he didn't have to repeat it. Because, of course, she'd heard him perfectly well.

Her hair swung around her chin as she shook her head. Hard. "No. No, there can't be a fire. I didn't use the stove for breakfast before we left this morning. I didn't leave a curling iron on." Then, she realized that he was slowing the truck on the deserted highway, preparing to pull a U-turn. "Why are you turning around?"

"To take you back to my place."

"No!" She grabbed his arm and the truck lurched unevenly. "We have to go to Weaver."

He straightened the wheels. "It's not safe." He didn't know that for certain, but until they knew the cause of the fire, he wasn't taking any chances.

"But it's my home!" Her fingertips dug even harder into his arm. "Please, Axel."

He made the mistake of looking at her.

At the sheen of tears he could see in her eyes.

He muttered a low oath and stood on the brakes and the truck fishtailed to a jerking stop. "Max said your house is fully engulfed. There's nothing you're going to be able to race in and save." Not her jewelry-making materials. Not her neatly squared magazines. Not her clothes or her books or that lonely photograph of her and her brother as kids with their parents that she kept on her dresser.

"Please, Axel."

It was just one more sign that he was a piss-poor agent when he couldn't withstand her soft, choking plea.

With a ripe curse, he reached past her for his glove box, yanking out his holster.

She went still, watching as he worked off his coat, fastened on the holster, then pulled the coat on again.

"You do have a gun." Her voice was small.

"And I hate carrying it. Which is why I'd just as soon go back to my place." He shoved the truck into gear and pulled back onto the road. Toward Weaver.

She finally spoke when they could see the pinpoints of light ahead of them. "Thank you."

"You won't be thanking me for long."

They could smell the smoke from blocks away. But he knew the true horror didn't hit Tara until he turned down her street.

Fire trucks were parked everywhere, their flashing beacons strobing over the windows of the nearby houses. Fat hoses pulsed and snaked along the sidewalk, over melting snow and winter-dead lawn, wielded by firefighters in helmets and heavy gear. Waves of billowing, cloying smoke rose from the remains of Tara's house.

"Oh my God," Tara whispered. She pressed her palms to her stomach as he slowed the truck to a crawl. She looked ill. "There's nothing left." She coughed into her hand.

Axel pulled to a stop well behind the barricade set up by the sheriff's cruisers. When she reached for the door handle, he caught her arm. "You can't go out there."

"It's my *house.*"

He didn't let go. Would have pulled her right into his arms, if he thought she'd have let him. "I know. But you still can't go out there. I shouldn't have even brought you this close."

"And I shouldn't have been with you!" Her voice filled the cab of his pickup. "If I'd have been here—"

"—you might have been caught inside," he finished, his voice flat. "Tara. I know this is hard. But *think.*"

She gulped down a choking breath. "Nothing ever stays the same. No matter what I do, everything always changes." She stared again through the windshield. "Just once, God, just once, why can't things just…stay…put?"

"Not everything changes." His hand cupped the back of her neck. "It's going to be all right, Tara."

She laughed brokenly. "How?" She gestured toward the wreckage of her house. "There's nothing left!"

She was right. Nothing was left but a stinking, swimming miasma of soot and debris. And still, arching streams of water jetted over it all from the fire hoses.

"Do they have to wash away every last reminder that it ever existed?"

He couldn't help it. He tugged her close. Pressed his lips to her forehead. "They don't want it to spread to the neighboring houses," he said quietly.

Her face crumpled again and she pulled away.

Axel put the truck in gear and began backing away from the melee only to stop when he saw Dee Crowder waving madly at them. She darted over the yard across from Tara's, her robe flapping behind her and her curly hair bouncing.

He rolled down his window when she reached the truck and the cloying smoke rolled inside. "Dee—"

"Oh, thank God." She pressed her head to the side of his truck for a minute. "One of the firemen said there was nobody in the house, but—" She shook her head again, then lifted the collar of her robe to her nose, trying to block out the horrible smoke. Her gaze bypassed Axel.

"Tara." She moved the robe again away from her mouth. "If there is *anything* I can do." She shook her head, looking back at the house for a moment. "I just can't believe it. Nobody can. Cynthia's going around the neighborhood. Gathering up some things we know you'll need just to get you through for a few days. I've got a spare bedroom, too. If you need a place to stay…or…well, I imagine that's not going to be necessary."

"Thanks, Dee," Axel answered when Tara just stared mutely at Dee.

She reached in and squeezed his hand, her smoke-reddened eyes looking from Tara's shell-shocked face to Axel. "Should I get the stuff out to your folks' place?"

"That'd be good, Dee. Thanks."

Dee nodded. Squeezed his arm once more, before stepping off the running board of his truck. She returned to the far side of the street where onlookers were clustered around, watching the goings-on with equal measures of shock and morbid fascination.

He closed the window and continued inching his way out of the congested street.

"Where are we going?" Tara's voice was dull.

"Back to my place."

She didn't argue.

He would have felt better if she had.

She was silent until they reached his cabin. "Your cousins are still here."

Sure enough, Casey's truck was still there. "They won't be for long." He went around to open her door but she'd already slid from the high seat, her skirt trailing behind her.

He took her arm and guided her inside.

One look at Tara's face and both of his cousins put down their pool cues.

He lifted a hand toward them. "In a minute."

He walked Tara into his bedroom and nudged her onto the side of his bed. When she made no move to remove her coat, he leaned over her and did it himself.

"That place was supposed to be temporary." Her voice was raw. "So why does it hurt so much?"

He crouched at her feet and pulled off her boots. "Maybe because you've lived there longer than anywhere else."

She didn't reply as she silently tipped backward onto the pillows.

Worry was a hard, painful knot in the pit of his stomach as he settled his quilt over her. "Do you want me to stay with you?"

She turned her head further into the pillow. "No."

He exhaled. Uncurled a clenched fist and lifted it to brush her tangled hair away from her pale, exhausted face. But he stopped the motion midair.

If he'd been doing his job the way he was supposed to have been, if he hadn't let himself get distracted by her, he might have prevented the fire.

Might have caught the bastard who'd set it and they could have put an end to this whole mess.

"Just rest" is all he said, moving silently out of the bedroom to pull the door nearly closed.

Jaws tight, he went into the kitchen—the room farthest from his bedroom. Casey and Erik followed.

"I've already heard," Erik said, holding up his cell phone. "That was Dad. He's been trying to reach you."

Axel bet Tristan was, too. "My phone's in the truck."

"Is there anything we can do?" Casey asked.

"Tell your dad to keep a shotgun handy," he muttered, entirely serious. If a person drew a line between the farm, the Double-C and Daniel and Maggie's place, it was almost a perfect triangle, with Axel's cabin squarely between, as snug as a protected child.

"It's like that, then," Erik said, doing a reasonable job of trying to hide his shock. He had yet to feel the Hollins-Winword itch, despite the fact that his father, Tristan, was about as deep in the agency as it was possible to get.

"Yeah. It's like that."

Casey nodded solemnly. He, too, had avoided the agency's lure. His interest was literature and ladies. But he was also one of the best shots in the family. His father, Daniel, had taught him well. "You want us to keep post around here?"

Axel scrubbed his hand down his face. His father could put the ranch hands on alert on the horse farm side. Matthew could do the same on the Double-C side. "Keep anyone from getting past your dad's place. And for God's sake, don't talk about any of this to an outsider." He knew the reminder was needless, but made it anyway.

His cousins nodded and immediately headed out.

Axel quietly went back to the bedroom, peering around the door. Tara had turned on her other side. He couldn't see her face. Nor could he hear her crying. Her tears would have been easier to take than her numb silence.

He went out to his truck and retrieved his cell phone. Ignoring the messages that were waiting, he dialed his father.

"We've heard," Jefferson answered immediately. "Where are you? Are you both okay?"

"The cabin. I'm okay." He pinched the bridge of his nose. "I'm not so sure about her."

"Max said the old place went up like a Roman candle. Anyone saying yet what caused it?"

Axel knew the fire department would do its own investigation, but considering the situation, it was too much to hope that the fire had been accidental. "Can you drive out here?"

"Yeah. I'll bring your mother."

"Good." There was nobody better in a crisis than Emily Clay. "How many hands you got around?"

He could practically feel his father absorbing that question, and coming to his own—typically accurate—conclusion about its subtext. "Enough," Jefferson said evenly. "We've got more than enough, son."

Then the phone went silent and Axel went into the living room. He started a fire in the fireplace. Stuck Erik's unopened root beer in the fridge and replaced the pool cues in the rack.

He listened to Tristan's furious phone messages.

Mostly, though, he thought about the woman in his bed and wished to hell that she was there for *any* reason other than this.

## *Chapter Fourteen*

"You're awake."

Tara eyed Axel's mother sitting in a wooden rocking chair not far from the bed. A small lamp on top of a packing crate offered the only light in the bedroom.

The rocking chair was just like the ones she'd imagined for Axel's front porch.

"Can I get you something? Water?" Emily's smile was gently wry. "Whiskey?"

Just that easily, Tara's eyes welled.

Emily clucked softly and set the book she'd been reading on the seat of the chair as she moved to the side of the bed. She brushed the hair back from Tara's face and cupped her chin. "It's all right," Emily soothed. "The important thing is that nobody was hurt."

That was true. But it was hard to feel all that blessed, when everything Tara personally owned had gone up in flames.

She swallowed hard, only to be gripped by a cough.

"I'll get you some water," Emily said. "I won't be a second." She quickly left the room.

Tara pressed her head back against the pillow. It smelled smoky. But then she realized it was *her* that smelled of smoke.

She lifted her arm, covering her eyes, and tried blocking out everything. The indistinguishable murmur of Emily's voice from the other room as she spoke to someone. The warm glow of the lamp in the otherwise dark room.

The fact that she was in Axel Clay's bed. A place where she'd tried for months to make herself believe she didn't want to be. Tried. And failed.

A flutter tickled low in her abdomen and she went still. Slowly dropped her arm and pushed up on her elbows, her palms creeping across her stomach.

And then she felt it again. A brush of butterfly wings. Her baby had moved.

"Here you go, Tara." Emily reappeared, holding out a glass of water.

Tara's hands slowly fell from her tummy and she sat up a little more, taking the glass. The water felt good against her raspy throat and she drank it all.

Emily took the glass when she was finished and set it on the carton next to the lamp, then picked up her book and sat down once more. "I'm just going to sit here for a while, all right?"

"How…how long have you been here?"

"Since Axel called us after he brought you back here. It's about 2:00 a.m. now."

Tara started. "You haven't been sitting there all that time?"

"Of course I have." Emily smiled slightly. "Axel didn't want you to wake up and be alone."

The woman's kindness was almost unbearable. "Where, uh, where *is* he?"

"He went to town with his father last night. Don't worry." Emily added. "Mason Hyde's been here every minute since."

Tara's lips parted. "You know about Mason?"

"I know about a lot of things," Emily assured her calmly. "Axel told us about your brother, dear."

The baby fluttered again. "I'm sorry," Tara blurted out. "I'm sorry we misled you."

"Misled?" Emily's eyebrows rose slightly, inquisitively, and Tara suddenly realized that Axel wasn't *quite* a carbon copy of his father, Jefferson. He'd inherited this exact look from his mother, as well.

"About," she continued and then swallowed again, "about being…involved."

Oddly enough, Axel's mother looked vaguely amused. "But you are involved."

"Only because he was *assigned* to me."

Emily set her book down again and moved back to sit on the side of the bed. "Jefferson and I weren't altogether pleased when Axel decided to do the work he does." She shook her head slightly. "But that desire inside him—to do what's right however he can—isn't just something he learned growing up in this family." She let out a soft laugh. "I think it was programmed into his DNA long before he—or his father—was born. But never—" she picked up Tara's hand in hers "—never, has he brought one of his *assignments* to Sunday dinner. In fact, he's never brought a woman at all to Sunday dinner." She squeezed Tara's hand. "You matter to my son. I've known it since he used to volunteer to drive me into town to visit your shop. That makes you matter to us, all that much more."

Tara wasn't ready to examine the notion that she'd held any interest to Axel before that night in Braden. But this kind woman was her child's grandmother. And that fact was staring her right in the face. "Emily—" she said and broke off, the words she wanted to say dammed behind years of reticence. "I've never met anyone like you. Your family." It wasn't at all what she *needed* to say.

The older woman smiled again. "We're just a family. Good, bad, occasionally quirky. But we pull together when we need to."

"My family wasn't like this."

"You have just your brother?"

Tara looked away. Not even her brother, anymore. Not really. "Our parents died in an auto accident almost ten years ago." A perfectly ordinary—if such a thing could be termed that—car accident. One that had nothing at all to do with the CIA, or the constant upheaval of their lives.

Just a drunk kid who was driving a stolen car. *Just.*

"That's how I lost my parents," Emily replied softly. "I was a child, though. Squire—he was a relation of sorts by marriage—brought me here to live with him."

"Then you were raised with—"

"Jefferson? Well, he *was* somewhat older, but yes." Emily squeezed her hand again, then let go. "But we can talk about that another time. Right now, you should try to get more sleep." As if Tara were no older than a child, she tucked the quilt over her, then moved back to the chair and her book. "I'll just sit with you for a while longer. Make sure you go to sleep all right. That is if the light won't bother you?"

"It doesn't bother me." Tara's voice was husky and not because of the smoke she'd inhaled. "Thank you."

Emily's eyes looked a little surprised. "For what?"

Tara told the bald, sad truth. "My mother didn't sit with me at night even when I was a little girl. That would have been…coddling, which my father didn't allow."

Emily's brows pulled together. "Oh, honey." She sighed a little. "Sometimes even a grown woman needs a little coddling." She sat forward, leaning over the book on her lap, toward the bed. "And you say you don't have your brother. But he's the one insisting on your protection. Whether he's with you or not, he's obviously concerned." Her hands spread. "Rightfully so, it appears."

Tara shook her head. "I've lived too long with Sloan's paranoia. The fire will turn out to be completely unrelated to him."

"Maybe you'll be right. Axel will probably have more answers in the morning. For now, just try and sleep."

"What about you?"

Emily's smile was gentle. "You can chalk it up to conditioning for when I get to help out when my next grandbaby is born."

Somehow, Tara managed a faint smile. And then she closed her eyes.

When she woke the next time, light was flooding through the unadorned windows opposite Axel's bed.

Tara looked around. The rocking chair was unoccupied; the lamp turned off. She leaned over and took the water glass that had been refilled and drank it right down.

The door to the bedroom was ajar, and she could hear the low murmur of voices. The only one she recognized, though, was Axel's.

She exhaled and pushed back the quilt. Aside from the bed, the only other furniture was the chair and lamp. And a stack of packing boxes. She didn't spot a clock anywhere, either.

She had no idea what time it was.

She looked out the windows opposite the bed and saw nothing but an expanse of snow, glistening under the bright sun, and a jut of craggy rocks beyond that. Axel's bedroom, she realized, overlooked a mountain base.

The bedroom possessed two doors—both closed—aside from the door leading out to the living area. She opened one and found a closet. A full closet.

Her fingertips drifted over the sleeve of a dark blue shirt. If she hadn't reeked of smoke, she would have pressed her face into the fabric. Instead, she closed the door and opened the other. Mercifully, it led to a bathroom.

A long, wood-framed mirror ran the length of one wall,

throwing her haggard reflection back at her. A single toothbrush sat in a stainless-steel holder and a single set of thick black towels hung on the rod next to a glass-walled shower. Feeling like a snoop, she opened a few cupboards, but most were empty. No extra towels, though she did find toothpaste and a disposable razor.

She peeled off her clothes, flushing over her absent panties, then reached in to flip on the shower which turned hot almost immediately. She stepped inside, trying not to think about her old claw-foot tub and slow water heater, because if she did, she'd start crying again.

He had a bottle of shampoo on a ledge built high into one slate wall, and a bar of soap. She snatched the soft washcloth from the towel rod, grabbed the nearby tube of toothpaste and the razor, and stepped beneath the comforting spray.

She washed her hair. Twice. Soaped her body. Scrubbed her face and rubbed toothpaste around her teeth until she no longer felt as though she'd swallowed a mouse. Then she unwrapped the razor and used that, too. Because she could have stayed in the steamy shower blocking out reality for about an eon, she made herself turn off the water and get out.

Her pile of clothing was right where she'd left it on the floor. Wrinkled, and smelling of acrid smoke.

She wrapped the towel around her torso, tucking the ends in above her breasts and stepped over the pile, pulling open the bathroom door. She'd wear something from Axel's closet before she'd put that skirt and sweater on again.

But the sight of him, sitting on the side of the bed with a huge plastic bag beside him, stopped her short.

Her hands went to the knot holding the towel together. "I, um, I took a shower." Then she flushed to the roots of her hair for stating the obvious. "I hope that's all right."

"I've been using your shower for a week. What do you think?"

"I think you look tired." He did. Older, grimmer, and more

worn than she'd ever seen him. The gray T-shirt he wore was smudged with black, and dried mud was caked on his boots and his jeans. "You haven't slept at all, have you?"

"I grabbed a few hours last night. A few of us picked through the debris this morning." She realized he was holding a much smaller bag when he held it out to her. "I'm afraid this is all we could salvage."

She slowly reached for the bag. Inside was her mother's hand mirror. The glass was cracked.

"We cleaned it up as best we could."

She sank her teeth into her tongue until she'd mastered the shaky sob that wanted to escape. "We?"

"My cousins. My mother. We all went out there."

She looked at him. At the deep gold hair that looked as if he'd been clawing through it. At the filthy state of his clothing, earned by trudging through the remains of her house. She tightened her fingers around the mirror. "You should have woken me."

"You needed sleep more than you needed to sift through ashes." He sighed deeply. "Maybe I needed to *not* see you having to sift through ashes."

Her throat tightened even more. She looked back in the bag and pulled out the narrow albums that she'd kept locked away. She rubbed her thumb over the rippled, blackened covers that had once been smooth leather.

"I found them in a metal foot locker," he told her.

"I kept it in the hall closet." She slowly opened one of the albums. The pages cracked as she turned them, but by some miracle, hadn't melted together.

She traced her fingertip gently over a faded black-and-white snapshot of her mother wearing a parochial school uniform. She carefully closed the cover and held the two albums against her heart. "Thank you." Her voice was thick.

"Don't thank me. If I'd been—" he said and broke off, exhaling sharply through his nose.

She very nearly reached out to touch him. "This wasn't your fault."

"It wasn't arson," he said abruptly. "The fire department ruled it accidental. Faulty wiring in the basement."

"Wiring," she echoed, stunned despite everything.

His hands clenched. "I wanted to keep your routine varied. Not head straight back to your house after you closed the shop every damned day. Turns out, if I hadn't finagled dinner at my folks', we'd have been at your place. Might have caught it earlier—"

"—and we might not have," she reminded him. "You said that yourself, Axel. But you could have told me that's what this was all about." She waved her hand. "Varying our routine, I mean."

"Making love to you was not about *varying*. It damn sure wasn't about my *job!*" He blew out another breath. "Here." He pulled open the top of the large bag sitting beside him. "My mother brought these by yesterday afternoon for you."

"Yesterday." She frowned. "But the fire was last night."

He shook his head. "You slept through the entire day, yesterday. It's Monday. Almost noon, in fact."

"But—"

He lifted his hand. "Don't say that the shop should be open."

Her gaping mouth closed. The shop, for once, had been the furthest thing from her mind. "I've never slept an entire day."

"You just did. I even called Rebecca to come over and check on you."

She went still. His aunt, Rebecca Clay, was the chief of staff at Weaver's small hospital. "What—" She had to stop and clear her throat. "What did she say?"

"That you were exhausted. In shock. And to let you sleep." He looked back at the bag. "Sarah's going to bring by everything that Dee and the rest of your neighbors collected for you after she's finished teaching for the day." He waved a hand. "But for now, you've got some clothes. Shoes. Personal...stuff. If there's anything else you need, someone'll get it for you."

Her nose itched. Her eyes burned. She carefully set the albums on the bed and looked in the bag, pulling out the blouse folded neatly on top. "Your mother bought this from me a few months ago."

"She's a few inches taller than you, but she figured some of her stuff would fit you. Leandra sent the boots and the tennis shoes."

Tara slowly unpacked the bag. Aside from more garments that she recognized from the shop, there were packages of socks, cotton panties, and spaghetti-strapped undershirts. "These are brand new."

"Leandra's doing. The other bag of stuff in there was her idea, too. She said what you carry in your shop is a lot nicer, but this stuff would get you by for a few days."

She'd already discovered the other "stuff." Small bottles of toiletries. Even a package of tampons.

She clutched the small box. "Why is everyone doing all of this? For me?"

"Why wouldn't they?"

"I don't deserve it." She dropped the box onto the pile and it slid off, tumbling to the floor. "I don't deserve any of this."

"No. You don't." His voice was as rough as his expression. "You didn't deserve to have that house of yours burn down while I wasn't looking."

"That's not what I meant. I meant, all of this." She waved her hand over the items she'd pulled from the bag. "Your family—*everyone* has been too generous. And I—" Her throat closed up. She looked at him, knowing she couldn't continue keeping the truth from him when it had been so wrong of her in the first place. "Axel—God. I'm sorry. I'm so sorry."

"For what?"

But her words—her thoughts—were tumbling over each

other in a race to expunge her horrible deed. "I should have told you. I should have found a way to reach you. Or at the very least, to tell you that first day, at the festival. I—"

He rose from the bedside and caught her arms. "Calm down. You should have told me what?"

But even staring into his frowning eyes, she couldn't make the simple truth come. "I—"

"Hey." He cocked his head to one side, his voice gentle. "Just tell me what's bothering you. We'll find a way to fix it."

She laughed brokenly and pulled his hand until his palm was pressed flat against her towel.

Against the swell of their child. "How do we fix this?"

He went still for an interminable moment.

Then with a sudden yank, he pulled the towel right away from her, flinging it to the side so she didn't even have a chance to snatch it back to cover her nudity.

"You're pregnant." His words dropped like stones in the room. His hand went back to her abdomen and she felt singed by the heat of his palm. "How?"

"The usual way." Her attempt at humor fell painfully flat. Because she couldn't bear it another moment, she grabbed the towel again, whisking it around her torso, but there was no concealing her naked nerves.

"We used condoms!"

"Obviously one of them failed!"

He scrubbed his hand down his face, moving around her to pace across the room. "I've been with you practically nonstop for a week." His voice rose again. "When the hell did you plan to tell me?"

Her guilty silence evidently spoke volumes and an oath escaped his clenched teeth. "You didn't *plan* to tell me." In two strides he was back to her, his hands hard on her shoulders. "At all?" He bit the words off.

"I...I thought it would be best." Even to her, it sounded paltry.

He looked furious. "For *who?* You?"

"For the baby. I didn't want my child to have the same kind of childhood I'd had!"

A muscle ticked in his tight jaw. "Yeah. Fine. But you didn't know what I did for a living until I told you. So what about the four freaking months between that weekend in Braden and when I came to you nine days—" the word was like a whip, cracking across her conscience "—ago?"

She winced, because she didn't have anywhere near a good enough reason for her silence.

"I didn't know where you were," she reminded him. "You certainly weren't in Weaver. And you certainly weren't making any attempt to contact me. For all I knew, that weekend was the only thing you were interested in. And when you came to me at the Valentine's Festival, the only reason you did, was because of Sloan!"

"You knew where my parents were. Where practically my entire family is! Did you think to ask *them* how to reach me?"

Her vision blurred with hot tears. "I told you I was sorry. What more do you want me to say?"

He let her go again, hissing out a breath between his teeth. "It might be too late to make it to the courthouse today. If it is, we'll go in the morning."

She swiped her cheeks. "The courthouse?"

"For a marriage license." He strode toward the bedroom door, casting a burning glance at her as he went.

"A *marriage* license," she echoed, stunned right out of her senses. "Wh-what for?"

"Because no child of mine is going to be born to a woman *not* my wife," he said flatly. His gaze burned over her. "Get dressed. We've got things to do."

Then he stepped out of the bedroom, closing the door with a silence that was far more effective than if he'd simply slammed it shut.

## *Chapter Fifteen*

"I have an obstetrician already," Tara told Axel—after she'd come out of her shell shock and put on some clothing—when he dragged her into Weaver. But instead of the courthouse, he'd brought her to the hospital.

His hand was like iron around her wrist, brooking no disagreement as their heels rang against the tile corridor. "I want Rebecca to examine you."

"She saw me last night. You told me so, yourself."

"She didn't *examine* you." He stopped short in the hallway, not seeming to care in the least that there were two nurses nearby, or that Mason Hyde was within earshot, maintaining a not-so-discreet distance between them. "And why would she think she needed to? Why would any of us have thought that, considering the *detail* that you decided I didn't need to know about?"

She tugged at her wrist. "You're making a scene."

"And God forbid we do that." He didn't let go of her, but started walking again, his strides so long that she had to jog to keep up with him. Finally, he came to a closed door and after a peremptory knock, pulled Tara right inside.

Rebecca was sitting at her wide desk. "What's—"

"She's pregnant," Axel announced baldly.

If Axel's physician-aunt was surprised, she hid it well as she closed the medical file she'd been reading. "How many weeks?"

"Four months of weeks," Axel answered again.

Rebecca's gaze slid to Tara.

"Almost eighteen weeks," she clarified. "And I have an OB in Braden."

"One that *I* don't know," he returned evenly. "One that I damn sure know you haven't seen in the past week."

"Axel, why don't you have a seat?" Rebecca's voice was calm. She moved the pile of charts to a drawer and extended her hand toward the doorway behind her. "Tara?"

The second they were closed in the adjoining examining room, Tara turned to the other woman. "I really *don't* need an exam. I'm fine. The baby's fine. Moving even."

"I'm sure you're right," Rebecca said, still managing to slide off Tara's coat and guide her to the exam table where she immediately slipped a blood pressure cuff around her arm. "But I think my nephew may need a moment or two to cool his heels. And you have had a shock, lately. We're all so sorry about your house."

Tara let out a shaky breath. It seemed unfathomable that the house had dropped so low on her list of worries. "Thank you. It's still hard to believe."

"I can understand that," the other woman murmured. She slid the cuff off again. "So who is your OB?"

Tara told her and Rebecca nodded. "Good choice. Braden's a little far from Weaver when it comes time for delivery, though." Her head tilted a little, her eyes friendly yet professional. "Have you thought about that?"

"It's months away, yet."

"You're almost halfway to term," Rebecca reminded her gently. "The time might pass more quickly than you expect. But—" she said as she smiled faintly "—it's your decision entirely."

"Axel doesn't think so."

"The baby is his, I take it."

Tara gnawed the inside of her lip. Tugged the hem of her borrowed T-shirt further down over the jeans she'd had to roll up so they wouldn't drag on the ground. "Yes."

"Well." Rebecca patted her knee and sat down on the low, rolling stool. "What you and I say in here is between us, despite what Axel might think. But I may as well warn you—from experience—that when it comes to the Clay men, they take their parental responsibilities very seriously. He's undoubtedly going to want to be part of every decision that you make."

"So I've noticed."

"Mmm. So, any dizziness? Nausea? Spotting?"

Tara shook her head. "I feel fine. Truly." Then she made a face. "My prenatal vitamins went up in flames."

"At least they're replaceable," Rebecca said. She wrote out a prescription and handed it to Tara. "They can fill it in the pharmacy here."

Tara folded the small square of paper. "Thank you."

"Anything you're worried about? Any questions?"

A host of them, none of which concerned the health of her pregnancy. She shook her head.

"All right, then." Rebecca reached for the door and sent her a conspiratorial wink. "Let's go brave Axel."

He was pacing when they rejoined him in Rebecca's office. He'd taken off his coat, revealing the gun holster he'd put on before leaving his cabin. Despite the accidental ruling where the fire was concerned, he was making no bones that he planned to be even more vigilant where she—and *his* baby—were concerned. "Well?"

"Well," Rebecca said as she went over to her nephew and pressed a kiss to his cheek, evidently unfazed by the sight of his weapon, "first of all, congratulations."

His smile looked oddly bleak. "Thanks. She's okay though?"

"Nothing that another five months won't cure," Rebecca replied with a smile. "Now go on. I have to get through my charts."

Axel yanked on the shearling coat that made his wide shoulders massive, and grabbed Tara's hand again, as if he expected her to race away from him.

"I'm not going to run," she told him under her breath. "You can let go of the shackle."

He did no such thing, though. Not when they stopped at the pharmacy, not when they went back out to his truck that he'd left parked in the red zone, and not when they drove to the courthouse, where he parked just as illegally before practically carrying her through the front door.

Somehow, he managed to get through the security check without surrendering his gun or Tara's wrist, but outside the office with a big *Marriage* placard above the door, Tara finally succeeded at digging in her heels. "Axel, this is wrong."

"People should be married before they bring a baby into the world," he said inflexibly.

They should both be in love, too, she thought bleakly. "This is only going to complicate things. I've already said the marriage vows once, for *all* the wrong reasons. And it lasted all of a month."

"You were both eighteen," he said flatly. "Kids who didn't know what they were doing, or what they wanted out of life."

He shoved open the office door and tugged her inside where, at last, he let go of her wrist. "You told me yourself how you eloped straight out of school with some kid you barely knew." He leaned on the desk dividing the chairs from a small back area. "Anyone here?"

"Be right with you," a voice called back. "If you need a license, forms are on the clipboard on the desk."

Axel flipped the clipboard around to face him and began filling out the form. "What's your middle name?"

"I'm surprised you don't already know." She sounded churlish, but couldn't help it.

He slanted her a look.

"Beth."

He rapidly scratched the pen across the page. "Birthdate?" His lips twisted. "October 26," he answered for himself.

She cursed the heat that rose in her face. Of course he would remember *that* particular detail.

She edged closer, looking around his wide shoulder. "There's no point in filling that out," she told him in a low whisper. "We should not get married."

He scrawled his signature at the bottom of the form he'd completed in record time, then held the pen toward her. "Sign it."

"You don't love me." And she was very much afraid she loved him. Had since he'd told her to make a wish and blow out a few birthday candles.

*"Sign it."*

She snatched the pen. Signed her name and felt dizzy afterward. What was she doing?

"Okay now." A wizened little man with about three strands of hair pulled across his bald pate, rubbed his hands together as he pulled out the seat behind the desk. "Oh, hey there, Axel. I was just about ready to close up for the day." He eyed Tara with a frown. "Real sorry to hear about the fire, miss. Real sorry."

"Thank you."

The little man pulled the license application off the clipboard and began typing it up on an ancient typewriter. "You want to pay the fee in cash or credit card?"

Axel handed over several bills from his wallet when the

clerk finished and the man grinned, plainly oblivious to the strain between them as he slid the document into an envelope and handed it to Axel. "Best wishes to you, now."

"Thanks, George." Axel grabbed the envelope and hustled Tara to the door.

Another parking ticket awaited them. He yanked it from beneath the wiper blade and shoved it into the glove box where it was plainly in ample company.

"How many tickets do you *have?*"

"Maybe you'll be lucky and I'll be hauled in on parking violations before you have to eke out an *I do.*" He wheeled out of the parking lot like the devil was at their heels and she grabbed the dashboard to keep from swaying.

"That's one way of solving this," she said, "get us killed in a car accident!"

He slowed enough to give her a look. "The *only* reason I chanced bringing you into town was to get this—" he lifted the envelope holding their marriage license "—taken care of, and to get you looked at by my aunt. Now, we're going back to my place because, in case you've forgotten, though that fire might have been ruled as accidental, someone is after your brother, and maybe *you,* too!"

She clamped her lips shut and stared out the window. They whizzed past the front of her darkened shop and she debated asking him to drive her by her house, but quickly dismissed the idea. He'd have refused, and she wasn't sure she was ready to see the carnage again yet, anyway.

Instead, she tried for reason. "Marrying because of this baby is all wrong, Axel. Surely you can understand that."

"There are worse reasons."

"But you don't love me!"

"And you don't love me."

She looked away.

"You've got two choices, darlin'," Axel said after they

turned onto the highway. "And that's deciding between a judge and a minister. Because by the time we get back to my place, the news that we've gotten a marriage license will have been fully broadcasted."

"And the reason *why* you insisted on it?" Her voice was tight.

"That's going to be pretty evident the second you stop wearing clothes that hide that baby bump you've got going."

She crossed her arms defensively. "You don't even know that the baby is yours," she taunted.

He gave her a long, searing look. "You told me yourself you hadn't been with anyone since you were married. You were practically still a virgin, Tara, and God knows you haven't had anyone around since then. That baby is *mine.*"

She glared at him. "I think I detest you right now."

"Backatcha." His jaw was practically white. "But if I stopped this truck right now and touched you, you and I both know that we'd be all over each other."

"Don't be so sure."

He reached in his pocket and drew out a hank of pale pink lace. "Look familiar?"

She snatched at the lace panties, but he jerked them out of her reach. "I don't know what you're keeping them for."

"Fond memories." His voice was anything but fond, though, as he shoved the torn lace back into his pocket.

She fumed for the rest of the drive out to his cabin where she counted six—*six!*—vehicles parked in front.

She pushed open the truck door and stomped ahead of him through the trampled snow.

But before she could reach the door, Axel scooped an arm around her and hauled her back against him. "Put a smile on your face," he whispered above her ear.

She twisted, painfully aware of his arm just below her breasts. If anyone were looking out a window at them, it would look as if he were nuzzling her neck. "I won't."

"You will." His voice was hard. "Because there's not a soul in that cabin right now who deserves your animosity."

He couldn't have said anything more effective at draining her righteousness out of her.

The Clays—with the exception of Axel—had been nothing but kind to her. Her baby—*his* baby—was a Clay, too. Another part of that large, caring clan.

No matter what happened between her and Axel, there was no disputing that fact.

She stopped struggling against his arm. "You're right," she whispered.

His arm loosened and slowly fell away from her.

Ironically, she felt cold without it.

He pushed open the door and ushered her inside. And the moment they appeared, a horde of gleeful banshees descended upon them. From Axel's parents to his cousins, his sister, even a few aunts and uncles.

Slapping Axel on the back. Showering kisses on Tara's face. Popping open bottles of champagne and sparkling cider, claiming that they knew all along that Axel and Tara were headed for the altar. And the crowd just seemed to grow. As the afternoon slid into evening, more family arrived, bearing platters of food and buckets of beer bottles, folding chairs and folding tables.

The women chattered and the men shot pool and just as Axel had warned, the senior men gave as good as they got. But then Leandra and Sarah butted in and made a respectable showing themselves while Squire, sitting in a chair nearby, issued pointers to them. Something that the guys seemed to consider cheating.

It would have all been so perfectly perfect, if Tara hadn't known the only reason behind it all.

First, Axel had only returned to her because of his job. Now, he was only marrying her because of the baby.

Emily, carting a sleepy Lucas on her shoulder, stopped next to Tara where she was watching. "Do you play pool? Poker?"

"No on both points, I'm afraid."

Emily grinned. "Well, if you ever want to change that, just give a whisper in Squire's ear. He loves nothing better than an underdog." She swayed, patting the little boy's back. "Have you thought about your wedding dress?"

Tara's lips felt frozen. "Um…no."

But the mere mention of the words *wedding dress* was like waving a magnet to all the women in the room. They clustered around Tara and Emily.

"Have you set a date?" someone asked.

"What about flowers?" someone else asked.

"Music?"

"Attendants?"

The questions swirled around her until she wanted to press her hands to her ears. All she could do was helplessly spread her hands. "I don't know."

"A week from Saturday," Axel said, cutting through the throng to slide his hand around Tara's hip, which he squeezed in warning. "We know what we want and don't intend to wait."

Emily looked truly startled. "It takes a little time to plan a wedding, Axel. That's only twelve days from now!"

His lips curved. "I know the women in this family. They could create a world in ten."

Emily swatted him with her free hand. "Don't be smart. What if the church isn't available?"

"Then we'll get married somewhere else. Hell, I don't care if we do it on the football field."

Tara managed not to wince. He sounded as if he were simply anxious to marry her. But she knew his motives; knew that he couldn't possibly care about the ceremony.

"If twelve days is the case," Emily said, "then we'll have to be organized. Jaimie, get some paper."

"Got it." Jaimie ripped a brown paper bag that had carried a jug of milk and waved it over her head. "I need a pen."

Maggie slid one out of her purse and handed it to her sister-in-law.

"Okay." Emily went into commander mode. "Who has Reverend Stone's home number?"

"I do." Gloria pulled out a cell phone and started scrolling through numbers. "I've been helping him get his mother settled in an assisted care facility. Where is it—oh. Here." She reeled off the number and Jaimie duly noted it on her brown paper.

"Axel, go call him now," Emily suggested. "There's no time to waste."

Oddly enough, Tara wanted to grab him, keep him from moving away from her and leaving her to the mercy of this well-intentioned wedding mob.

But Emily, handing Lucas off to Jefferson, tucked her arm through Tara's. "Now, do you have something in your shop that you'd like to wear? Or, if you want, we could make a quick trip to Gillette. Casper. Cheyenne. Try the stores there."

"We could alter one of our dresses," Sarah chimed in. "Or even make a new one. Between Max's mother, Genna, and Leandra's mother-in-law, Jolie, they could whip together something remarkable in no time at all. They're both whizzes with a needle. And Braden has a wonderful fabric shop."

"What do you think, dear?"

Tara realized that all eyes seemed to have fallen on her. "I think I'm a little overwhelmed," she said faintly.

"Of course you are," Emily said comfortably. "Honestly. Men can be in such a rush, sometimes, and my son is no different. But don't worry. It'll all come together because Axel isn't all that wrong. When we put our minds to it, we can accomplish amazing things."

And several hours later when the celebratory mob started its exodus, Emily had proven herself right.

The church was confirmed. So was the florist. And the photographer. Even the menu had been hammered out for the reception, which would be held in the new barn Matthew had just built at the Double-C.

"The only thing you need to do is take care of the rings, and decide about your dress," Emily said. She and her husband were on the tail end of the departing mass. "I know Axel has a decent suit in his closet already from Ryan's service last year, though he might not want to wear it for a wedding."

"Mom." Axel closed his hands over his mother's shoulders and steered her toward the door where Jefferson was waiting. "I promise not to embarrass you by showing up in jeans and a dirty sweatshirt. Take her home, Dad, before she needs a horse tranquilizer to dial down."

"I can't help it." Emily hugged her son once more, then Tara. "I'm just more delighted than I could say. You're a perfect couple."

"Well, there's one thing more you oughta know," Axel said.

Tara opened her mouth to stop him, but it was too late. His arm had already slid around her waist again, totally proprietary as his hand flattened against her belly. "Tara's pregnant."

Emily's eyes widened slightly and Jefferson's narrowed.

"We'd be getting married immediately anyway," Axel added, and Tara quailed at the absolute lie.

"Of course you would," Emily said, pressing her hand to her heart. She hugged her son again. "*You* are going to be a wonderful father. And *you*," she said as she cupped her hands around Tara's face, "are going to be a wonderful mother. And daughter." She practically sailed out the door, while Jefferson shook his son's hand and clapped him on the back.

Then the man's vivid gaze turned on Tara. His smile was slow and gentle and so much like Axel's that it made her heart ache. "It might not be official for another twelve days," he said, "but welcome to the family."

And then the door closed behind them all, leaving Tara alone with Axel. "Don't even start," he warned, before she could open her mouth.

She winced. "You can't force me to marry you, Axel." Not even if she'd been weak enough to have signed the marriage license.

"No. I can't." He looked utterly weary. "But you're going to marry me, anyway. Because *that* family—" he said pointing toward the front door "—is going to provide *this* child with exactly what you can't seem to get over never having had yourself. You want roots? Well, sweetheart, the roots my family set into this earth are real and lasting. That's my baby you're carrying, and like it or not, you're part of them now, so I suggest you start getting used to the idea and stop pushing away the very things you claim to want."

"I don't do that," she defended herself shakily.

"Yeah." His voice was flat. "You do." Then he turned on his heel and disappeared into his bedroom only to return a moment later with a pillow that he tossed on the wide, leather couch.

"Take the bed," he said.

She hesitated. "But—"

"Fine. Stay out here, then. But we're going to do one of two things if you do. Argue. Or make love." He ripped his T-shirt over his head, balled it up and threw it aside. "More likely, we'll do both."

She shuddered, dragging her traitorous gaze from that wealth of sculpted flesh and sinew, and fled.

## *Chapter Sixteen*

The slam of the bedroom door echoed through the cabin. Axel sank down on the couch and raked his fingers through his hair, then looked at his hands.

They were shaking, God help him.

He pushed off the couch and paced around the room that showed only remnants of the celebration that had just been there.

How could she have kept it to herself? It was *his child* she was carrying!

He realized he'd stopped in front of the pictures they'd hung. Ryan's grinning mug stared back at him. Axel's jaw tightened and before he knew what he was doing, he slammed his fist square into the glass.

It shattered.

The surrounding frames shook. One fell off its nail and shattered when it landed.

He stared down at the explosion of shards littered around his boots.

"What did you do?" Tara's voice was soft. Shocked. When he didn't respond—couldn't seem to find his voice anywhere in the emotion yanking his guts to pieces—she crossed the room toward him.

The sight of her stocking feet approaching finally loosened his tongue. "Don't. You'll cut yourself."

She kept right on walking toward him, though.

Proving that he couldn't even protect her from some broken glass.

"You've cut *your*self," she countered. But she stopped shy of the circle of glass. "I knew it would have been better to use proper hangers than just those nails."

The nails had been working fine until he'd decided to use one of the pictures as a punching bag. "Go back to bed, Tara," he said wearily. "I'll clean this up."

"Do you have a broom?"

"In the mudroom off the kitchen. I'll get—"

But she was already heading out of the room.

He stared at the crooked pictures. Slowly righted the one of his parents in the center.

Tara returned with the broom and dustpan and silently began sweeping up the debris.

"I said I'd do it."

She ignored him, merely kneeling down to wield the dustpan. Then she straightened and carried everything back into his kitchen.

He eyed his parents' image.

All of his life he'd been trying to live up to the Clay name. To do what was right.

And now he was forcing a woman toward the altar who clearly didn't want to go there, and was maintaining the worst lie he could possibly think of when it came to his family.

He looked away from the picture only to spot Tara returning. This time she had a dish towel in her hand.

Her dark gaze avoided his when she stopped next to him. "Here." She reached for his hand and pressed the towel gently against his knuckles. "You're bleeding."

Maybe it was his own shock. Or the soft scent of her. Maybe it was just the weight of his own secrets that he couldn't bear. "Ryan's alive," he said baldly.

She froze. Slowly looked up at him, confusion knitting her eyebrows together over her fine nose. She cast a quick glance at the ruined photograph that was still, oddly enough, hanging by a nail. "Your cousin?"

His jaw was so tight it ached. "Yeah."

"How do you know?"

"Because I spent the past year tracking him down. Because that's where I went when I left you in Braden. I'd gotten a lead on him."

If anything, she looked even more confused. "Sit down," she said, and somehow he found himself nudged down onto the couch. She sat beside him, keeping his towel-wrapped hand tucked in her lap. "Now, start from the beginning."

There was no condemnation looking at him. No anger. No hurt. Nothing but those wide brown eyes that he'd lost himself in that night in the Suds-n-Grill when she'd blurted out that it was her birthday.

So he went to the beginning.

From the time when Ryan had first gone missing, ostensibly while on a naval assignment. To the months, then the years that had passed until Ryan's parents had finally, grievously, accepted the fact that their son was never coming home again.

"Everyone who knew anyone used their contacts to try to find Ryan." His lips twisted. "To bring his body home. Sawyer went back to his cronies from his navy days. My father. Tristan. They turned over every damn rock."

"Tristan," she repeated faintly. He saw the realization dawn on her. "*He*'s the not-so-distant uncle, isn't he? Good Lord,

Axel. How many people in your family are involved with Hollins-Winword?"

"Nobody as deeply as he is. Not anymore, at least."

She seemed to absorb that. "Then how did you find Ryan when nobody else had been able to?"

"It wasn't because I'm better at what I do than they were," he said flatly. "But Ryan and I were best friends. I had some idea of the assignment he'd been on and I never could swallow the official line that he'd been killed in the line of duty. So about the time everyone here was recovering from his memorial service, I was putting tails on his old contacts. And four months ago—" his fist tightened beneath the dish towel "—make that about eighteen weeks ago, I got a text message on my phone that I'd gotten a hit."

"That's why you were gone before I woke up that morning." Her voice was nearly soundless.

"I traced Ryan to Bangkok. He's living there—if that's what you want to call it—under an assumed name. I spent four months trying to convince him to come home. He swore he'd go even deeper to ground if I even considered telling the family that he was alive. God only knows what's driving him—but it's got to be something terrible. He wouldn't say." He didn't have to close his eyes to remember the cold hollowness in Ryan's eyes. "It was dumb luck that I found him in the first place. I didn't want to take that chance again, so I promised I'd stay quiet and he promised he'd check in through an e-mail service that's so bloody generic, he can disappear among the rest of the world that uses it."

"This is what you think you failed at?"

"Think?" He shook his head. "I *know*. I should have been able to talk him back to us."

"Oh, Axel." She pressed her forehead to the towel around his hand for a moment. When she straightened, her eyes were moist. "I know you. You'll keep trying. But you can't force your cousin to care any more than I can make Sloan care."

"Ryan cares," he assured her gruffly. "He cares too much. That's the only thing that makes a man turn away from what matters most. Same thing with Sloan."

But she shook her head and her silky hair swayed against her jaw. "If Sloan cared, he would have been at the Suds-n-Grill that night. 'We'll celebrate our birthday together,' he'd said. 'Like old times.' But he didn't care." Faint color bloomed on her high cheekbones. "The only celebrating I did was with you."

"He cared," Axel countered. "He just realized that I was the contact that Tristan had sent to meet him, and blew us both off as a result."

Her eyes widened. "You said you'd been stood up!"

"Yeah. By your brother. I was supposed to play courier for some information between Tristan and Sloan. A total of five minutes, tops, but I warned Tristan that your brother would turn the other direction the second he saw me. And that's exactly what he did."

She looked dazed. "I'm not sure I want to ask this...but *why?*"

He exhaled roughly. But what was the point in keeping the truth from her now? She already knew the worst about Ryan. She might as well know the worst about the rest.

"Nearly two years ago when Sloan came in from the gang, he brought a woman with him. Maria Delgado. She was a cocktail waitress at one of the Deuces' hangouts. They'd gotten involved and he didn't want to take any chances that the Deuces would retaliate against her because of him."

She let go of his hand and pushed to her feet. "What happened?"

"Sloan went to Tristan to ensure her protection and I got the detail. And she might have been just as crazy about Sloan at first, but the luster wore off pretty damn quick when she was in protective custody. I managed to keep her under rein for months before she succeeded in getting away from me. Unfortunately, she went straight back to the bar to try salvaging her damn job." His jaw tightened. "And I couldn't get there fast enough."

Her hand pressed against her rounded mouth.

"Her body was found a few days later. Your brother held me responsible. Rightfully enough. Tristan suspended me. I didn't care. My heart wasn't in it anymore. I was ready to resign by the time I went to the Suds-n-Grill that night in Braden. But I didn't, because—"

"—you received that text message about Ryan," she finished. She dropped her hand. Looked toward the ceiling. "I wish to God Sloan had never heard of Deuce's Cross." She let out a deep breath. Looked back at him. She was so pale, the faint freckles on her nose stood out like beacons. "Your hand is still bleeding." She knelt and folded the towel against his knuckles again.

He looked at the gleam of light catching in her deep brown hair. "Something good *did* happen."

"Like what?"

"I spent that weekend with you."

Her lashes lowered. "And look what happened." Her voice was soft. "We're lying even more to your family."

"Not all of it's a lie," he said gruffly. "You're having my baby."

She finally lifted her gaze again and tears sparkled on her lashes. "You were furious."

"Terrified," he countered roughly. "Not only do I need to keep you safe, I need to keep our child safe. And look how well I've done at keeping people safe!"

She dropped her cheek to his knee. "Oh, Axel. Not even you can protect everyone." Her voice was snowflake soft. "What are we going to do?"

"We're going to get married. We're going to raise our child. Together."

She didn't look at him. "What if it doesn't work?"

He couldn't help himself. He slid his fingers through the silky strands of her hair. "It will if we want it to."

She finally lifted her head, her eyes searching his. "Do you really believe that?"

He had to. "Yes."

"I don't even know where to start."

"Yes, you do." He closed his hands around her shoulders and drew her up toward him. "We start here. The same place we started before." He touched his lips to hers. She didn't resist. Didn't pull away. Just inhaled and slowly, slowly, lifted her cool fingertips to his face.

"A marriage isn't based on just sex," she whispered against him.

"This isn't just sex." He pulled her up even further until she was nearly in his lap. He tilted her face, looking straight into her eyes. "It's need."

She opened her mouth. But if she'd intended to protest, she never voiced it.

Instead, she leaned into him and pressed those soft lips, those soft breasts, that soft soul, against him. "Take me to bed, Axel."

And just that easily, everything inside him centered.

Holding her in his arms, he rose off the couch, lifting her right along with him. She clung, tucking her head into his neck, wrapping her legs around his waist.

He settled her on the side of the wide bed, then leaned over, pulling off her socks and tossing them aside. His fingers crept beneath the hem of her purple shirt, finding the waist of her jeans and realized that the button there was unfastened.

Instead of pulling down her zipper, he slowly lifted the shirt upward. She silently raised her arms and he tugged it away, his eyes taking in the lush swell of her breasts jutting tautly against her silky camisole.

Then his gaze dropped to the slight, but very distinct swell of her abdomen.

"How could I not realize?" He brushed his hand against her breasts; fuller than they'd been that night in Braden.

Her eyes were locked onto his face as if she were incapable of looking away. "You didn't know."

"I should have." Suddenly, he wanted—needed—to see more. Touch more.

He tugged the camisole over her head and color rose in her cheeks, rushed down her throat, bloomed across her breasts toward the rigid peaks that pouted up at him. When she went to shyly cross her arms over herself, he shook his head. "Don't. Don't hide from me. Not now."

Her arms subsided and he pulled the zipper of her jeans down and slowly, almost fearfully, settled his palms over that swell just below her navel. "When did you find out?"

"Not until nearly Christmas."

"Some Christmas present, huh?" he said gruffly.

"I don't regret it, Axel." Her fingers slid through his hair. "Not the baby. Not ever."

There was a burning deep inside his head. "Are you sure?"

"Positive." Her hands covered his, pressing them more firmly against her. "Feel that?"

What he felt was her velvety flesh and it was more than any mortal man could bear.

"The baby's moving."

He went still all over again as she guided his hand, seeming to follow in the trail of a wish he couldn't touch.

And then suddenly, he did feel it. Like a hummingbird's wings brushing against the palm of his hand.

He stared at her abdomen. "Amazing."

Her lips curved. Her eyes looked slumberous. "Yes."

She was female incarnate and the need raging inside him suddenly boiled over. He leaned over, tasting the fluttering pulse that throbbed at the base of her slender neck—oddly reminiscent of the flutter of the baby that he'd felt, only stronger. Headier.

He dragged his lips slowly along the path of that blushing color until he reached one nipple that beaded even more tightly beneath his lips.

She exhaled shakily and her fingers tightened spasmodically where they'd sunk into his hair. She nearly bowed off the bed beneath him.

Impatience reared and he tugged off her jeans. He felt sweat break out as he struggled not to fall on her like some starving beast. He was in danger of losing the battle altogether when her trembling fingers drifted down his chest, his stomach, finally stopping at his strained button fly.

The pearly white edge of her teeth sank into her lower lip and with an abrupt tug, she popped loose the top button. Her fingers moved against him as she struggled with the rest and he stifled an oath, taking over the task before he lost it completely.

"Wait." She suddenly scrambled off the bed. "We keep forgetting the boots." She pushed him all too easily onto the mattress and he nearly bit off his tongue as she bent over his feet, working them off.

It was a fine thing to realize that he was even aroused by the way she lined them up and set them neatly beside her shoes.

He caught her wrist and tugged her back to the bed, pulling her over him until her mouth was against his.

He swept his hands down the silky length of her spine; caught the creamy flare of her rear. Her sleekly taut thighs tensed against his before she moaned and slid her knees alongside his hips and with no pretense, no prevarication, took him deeply in.

He damn near saw stars in his head from the unearthly pleasure that rocked through him. She was wet and tight and wildly hot and with some portion of his mind he realized that he would never get enough of her. Never.

She was trembling, her brown eyes nearly black as her head went back and she cried out his name as she abruptly convulsed.

She was the most beautiful thing he'd ever seen.

And then she was collapsing forward, her breasts nestling against the hair on his chest, her hands weakly sliding over his shoulders, her tousled head finding a notch between his neck and his shoulder. "I'm sorry," she whispered over and over. "I couldn't wait. Again."

He nearly laughed, but there was just no laughter when his entire soul was ready to leap from him into her. He caught her hips, pulling her even closer. The clutching spasms deep inside her made his head spin.

He gritted his teeth, struggling for control. "I don't want to hurt you," he muttered. "Or the baby."

She lifted her head. Her slender fingers slowly settled against his jaw and she pressed her lips against his. "You won't hurt us," she whispered.

The trust in her wide eyes made his heart spin.

He slowly, carefully tipped her onto her back and her lips parted, her lashes nearly closing, as he settled into the cradle of her sweet hips and sank even more deeply.

Her hands raced up his chest, caught his shoulders and there it was again—that little gasp that had haunted his dreams for eighteen weeks.

And then, he couldn't think anymore as need insistently clawed through him, and he drew her hands down, slid his palms against hers, fingers tightening, flexing. Her legs tangled with his, her body rising to meet him, her gasps a soft counterpoint to the groan he couldn't withhold. And then she was crying his name again and they both tumbled headlong into that splintering heaven.

After a long while, when their bodies cooled and his heart

was beating back inside his chest where it belonged, and Tara was a softly sweet, sleeping weight against his side, he dragged the tangled bedding up over her shoulder and quietly slid out of bed.

The laptop that Tristan had provided to replace the one burned in the fire was sitting on the kitchen counter, the screen glowing in the dark room.

With a faint sigh, he logged in to the account he'd set up to communicate with Ryan.

The message he sent was brief and to the point.

*Getting married a week from Saturday. Need a best man.*

Then he shut the computer down and went back to bed.

Back to Tara.

## *Chapter Seventeen*

Tara stared at herself in the cheval mirror located inside the small bride's room of the Weaver Community Church and twitched the skirt of her tea-length gown. Despite a trip to Cheyenne with Emily, Leandra and Sarah to look for a dress there, she'd ended up choosing a buttery-colored vintage gown with a forgiving empire waist from her own shop. "Does it look all right?"

"It looks perfect. You're beautiful," Leandra assured her from over her shoulder. She was wearing a dove-gray sweater dress that hugged her still-slender figure from breast to knee.

"She's right," Sarah said, standing next to her cousin. Her strawberry-blond hair was twisted in a mass of curls on top of her head. "You look perfect."

There were other cousins there, too. Angeline, the curvaceous brunette who was married to a wryly humorous attorney named Brody. And J.D., the lanky blond horse trainer who'd arrived just that morning from Georgia. And then there was Lucy, the willowy ballerina from New York.

Once word spread that Axel was getting married, family began descending from every corner of the world.

The only one who hadn't shown his face was Ryan.

But Tara and Axel hadn't discussed him since that night at his cabin. They hadn't discussed Sloan, either, except to agree to ask Tristan to pass on their plans if he could reach Sloan.

"The music's starting," Lucy said now. "We should probably get seated. The church is already packed."

"Right." Leandra shooed the rest along and picked up the small bouquet of white peonies that the florist had miraculously produced. She was Tara's only attendant and had seemed terribly moved when Tara had shyly asked her. "I'll be waiting for you just outside the sanctuary."

Tara bit her lip. "Leandra—"

The other woman hesitated, her eyebrows lifting. "What is it?"

"Axel…he *is* here, isn't he?"

Leandra smiled. "Honey, he was the *first* one here."

Tara smiled faintly as if relief weren't flooding through her limbs. "I know that must sound silly."

"Axel's a good guy, Tara. He doesn't let people down. Particularly the people he loves."

"I know." She looked down at her skirt again. Except that Axel didn't love *her.* He cared about the baby, and he wanted Tara in his bed. He wanted to do what was right. He thought that would be enough to base a marriage on and she was too much in love with him to fight him anymore. When she thought she could manage a smile again, she looked up once more.

Leandra was smiling at her, but her eyes were concerned. "I know there's no replacing your own family, but I hope you know that we're all your family now, too."

Tara laughed a little brokenly. "Don't make me cry. My mascara will run."

"That's what tissues are for." Leandra snatched one out of the box sitting on the vanity by the window and handed it to Tara. Then she took one for herself and blew her nose. "See?" She quickly pressed her cheek against Tara's and headed for the door again. "Twenty minutes from now, this'll all be over and you'll be Mrs. Clay." She winked and closed the door behind her.

Tara went to the tissue box and pulled out another, dabbing her cheeks. Outside the window, the sky was a brilliant blue; the ground a pristine white. A dark-haired man jogged toward the church.

She smiled faintly. A last-minute guest.

From beyond the door, she could hear the strains of the organ.

Reverend Stone had already stopped by to make sure she was ready. Emily had stopped by to press a delicate hankie into her hands, telling her that she'd carried it when she'd married Axel's father.

The organ music was getting louder.

Tara took a deep breath. It might not quite be love on Axel's part, but it was on hers. So she picked up her own bouquet of peonies and reached for the door.

It wouldn't open.

She turned the knob the other direction. But still the door didn't budge. She set down her bouquet again and rattled the knob harder. It fell off in her hand.

"Oh, for heaven's sake." She crouched in front of the hole where the doorknob was supposed to fit and tried to work the post back inside.

The organist had finished the prelude and was now enthusiastically pounding out the first chords of the *Wedding March.*

Tara gave up on the knob and rose again, pounding her hand against the door and ignoring the faint knot in her stomach. Leandra would hear her and soon enough they'd be chuckling over the small mishap.

But a soft whooshing sound drew her attention around to the window opposite the door and the faint knot inside her exploded into a very large one.

Fire was creeping up the heavy drapes at the window and even in the split second it took to realize she wasn't seeing things, the flames rolled toward the ceiling.

Gasping, she turned to the door and slammed her hand against it in earnest, shouting. "Axel! Leandra!" She banged again and prayed that she was imagining the heat drawing closer to her. "Oh, God." She pressed her forehead against the door and screamed. "Axel!"

But there was no response.

She stared around the bride's room, looking for some other escape. But the only way was through the window, which was nearly engulfed by flames.

Should she throw something through the window? Her hands scrabbled over the wicker table and settee. They were too lightweight to break the glass. And she was afraid if she did manage to break the window, the rush of fresh air would feed the fire even more.

She dropped to her knees next to the door, sucking in harsh breaths, and banged with both hands on it.

"Tara."

She nearly sobbed with relief when she heard Axel's shout. The door vibrated against her cheek. "I can't get the door open!"

"Something's wedged in it," he said. "Move back."

She swiped her face. "Axel, the room's on fire."

"I know, honey. Just move to the side if you can and I'll get you out. The fire department's on the way."

She shoved the wicker settee away from the wall and stepped next to it.

A moment later, the door shuddered on its very hinges as something immense and heavy pounded against it.

The drapes were pillars of flame now. The smoke was beginning to fill the room. She could hear shouts from the other side of the door, and cried out when a shard of wood exploded inward from the solid door, followed by another. And another.

Her eyes were burning, but she recognized the tool he'd used to break through. A fire extinguisher.

Then his head poked through, his sharp gaze landing on her with naked relief. "Can you slip through here?"

She nodded, taking the hand he stuck through for her. She turned sideways and managed to work past the jagged wood but the hem of her dress caught and tore as he hauled her the rest of the way.

"Thank God." He swept her up against him.

She latched onto his waist. "It's a fire, Axel. Another fire. How—"

"We got the church evacuated," Evan shouted from the end of the hallway.

"Come on." Axel set her on her feet and pulled her along with him. He passed his brother-in-law, Evan, and they went into the empty sanctuary, closing the doors behind them. "We've got a few minutes before the fire can spread in here. Get in the pew. Keep your head down. Tristan's clearing the rear before I take you outside. The arsonist could still be near."

Too stunned to disobey, Tara slid into the pew next to him, staring at the ribbon tied at the end. "How'd you know to evacuate the rest?"

"Mason spotted the fire from outside. He went after the guy he thinks set it." Despite the fact that they were standing inside a church, Axel swore. "I *knew* the fire at your house had to be intentional." He yanked at the perfect knot of his paisley tie. "I've gotta get her out of here," he told Evan.

"That's for damn sure." Another deep voice cut across the sanctuary.

Tara sat up like a shot and stared at the source. "Sloan?"

Her brother looked like he'd aged ten years in the five that had passed since she'd last seen him. His hair was still the same brown as hers, but there were threads of silver in it now. She pressed her hand to her heart. "It's really you?"

"It's me." He didn't look at her though as he walked across the chancel. His hard gaze was on Axel. "I see you're doing your usual job of keeping people *safe.*"

Tara scrambled off the pew, dragging the hem of her torn skirt with her. "Don't go blaming Axel for this!"

"Maybe the family reunion should wait," Evan suggested, "since there's a fire burning close by?"

Axel took her arm and keeping her behind him, pulled her toward the front of the church and Sloan. "Where the hell have you been hiding?" he asked as they passed her brother.

"I've been on the trail of the bastard who burned down my sister's house," Sloan returned coldly. "While you've just been on her…trail."

Tara stopped short and stuck her finger in her brother's face. Axel let her go, moving ahead along the short hallway to the door at the end. "Don't," she warned. "Don't you dare judge anyone here, Sloan. You're the one who's brought this on our heads!"

For a moment, her brother looked pained. "Tara, you've gotta understand—"

"Tara," Axel called and she hurried over to him. "Tristan's outside with the car. Ten feet away. We're going to keep our heads down and run together and you're going to head straight inside the back seat. Okay?"

She shuddered, gripping his hand. Every doubt she'd ever had that someone might try to harm her had fled in the bride's room.

But she trusted Axel. He wouldn't let anything happen to her or their child. So she swallowed the panic clawing inside her and nodded. "Okay."

Axel opened the door and she crouched low, and found herself practically lifted off her feet as he bolted toward the car's opened door. Next thing she knew, she was sliding face first across the seat. The door shut behind her and she twisted around, gasping when she saw him disappearing right back into the church. "Where's he going?" she cried as Axel's uncle peeled away with a squeal of the tires.

"He's going back to catch who did this."

She leaned toward the seat between them.

"Keep your head down." Tristan's voice was sharp.

She wrapped her arms around her middle and immediately tucked herself into a ball on the seat.

"Max," she heard Tristan say, and realized he was on a radio. "You got the highway cleared?"

"Affirmative."

"Tara, did you see or hear anything before the fire broke out?"

"No. All I saw were wedding guests." She desperately wanted to lift her head and look out the window again. "Where are you taking me?"

"To the Double-C. It's as good as a fortress. You'll be safe there."

"Why didn't Axel come with me?"

"Because right now, he's doing what he needs to do."

She pressed her cheek into the leather seat beneath her. She wouldn't be able to bear it if anything happened to him. "He said I should think of you Hollins-Winword people as guardian angels."

Tristan made a muffled sound. A little like a laugh he was covering. "That's one way of looking at it."

The radio crackled again. "Shots fired," a disembodied voice reported. "Man down."

Tara bolted upright again. Her fingers dug into the seat in front of her. "What man?"

Tristan didn't so much as turn his head as he flipped off the radio. "Get your head down. *Now.*"

She lay down again. Tears leaked onto the seat beneath her cheek. *What man?*

She was no closer to an answer when they arrived at the Double-C. If terror hadn't tied her into knots, she might have been surprised by the number of people who'd beat them there. The second Tristan pulled up to a stop in the wide, circular driveway, the front door flew open and both Gloria and Emily hurried down the steps, folding her in their arms when she left the car.

"It's going to be all right," they kept saying as they drew her into the house where someone else tucked a crocheted afghan around her shoulders.

"I need to know who's been shot," she said distinctly.

Emily blanched. "Shot?"

Jefferson walked into the room, a rifle cradled in one arm. He slid his free arm around his wife. "Tristan is finding out what he can."

Tara stared at the weapon Axel's father was holding with such ease and felt her stomach curdle. She cast Gloria a desperate look and the woman quickly steered her to the bathroom.

Tara shoved the door closed and collapsed to her knees on the soft rug. But it wasn't nausea she succumbed to; it was tears. Tears that she hid in the fluffy towel she dragged off the towel rack.

Tears for the things she should have said.

The chances that she'd let pass.

Tears for the things that didn't matter a whit when the only man she'd ever loved was in danger because of her!

"Hey now." Eventually Emily slipped into the bathroom and ran her hand down Tara's head. "This won't do at all."

"I love him," she cried. "Why didn't I just tell him?"

"You will," Emily soothed. "But you're going to upset the baby, too."

Tara finally lifted her head. "If I had just left Weaver when he came to me, none of this would be happening."

Emily took the corner of the towel and blotted it against Tara's cheeks. "If you had left Weaver, I am quite certain my son would have been right behind you." She tossed the towel over the sink and straightened. "Now, come. Let's get you out of this torn dress. Then you can lay down for a while. Rest."

She didn't want to lay down. She didn't want to rest. She wanted to see Axel. To know for certain that he was all right. But she pushed to her feet and followed Axel's mother up the stairs.

A sudden commotion at the front door made her heart climb into her throat and she stopped on the landing, gripping the banister until her knuckles turned white.

And then, there he was.

Axel.

It seemed as if the world slowed on its axis as he looked unerringly up at her and slowly, purposefully headed for the staircase.

He didn't stop until he was only a foot away.

Her eyes raced over him. The sleeve of his suit coat was torn. The ends of his tie were sticking out of his pocket and there was a bloody stain on his white shirt.

Her hands unlocked from the banister and she reached for him. Ran her shaking fingers over the stain.

"It's not my blood," he assured her softly.

She threw her arms around his neck, clinging, and never felt anything as wondrous as when his arms closed around her, too. She pressed her face to his neck. "I would have died if something had happened to you."

"I'm fine." His arms were tight around her. "Mason and Sloan caught the guy. Your brother's been tracking him down since the fire at your house. It was Maria Delgado's brother." He held her even tighter. "Max has him locked up good and tight at the jail and he's wailing like a baby how he'd only wanted to make Sloan pay for Maria's death. He couldn't get to any of the Deuces, but when he put the word out about a hit, he knew it would be attributed to them." His hands ran down her spine. "He figured he'd get retribution and they'd take the blame. But it's all over. You won't have to worry anymore."

She couldn't make herself loosen her hold. "Is Sloan…is he okay?"

"He got nicked in the arm, but yeah. He's okay."

"Nicked!" She swayed a little.

"He'll be fine," he promised.

She believed him. Gratitude made her knees week. "What about the church?"

"There's some damage, but the fire department caught the blaze before it could spread to the sanctuary." He tilted her head back. "A couple of weeks and it'll be ready for another wedding."

He caught her hands in his, detaching them from their death grip around his neck. "But I realized something today when I was waiting for you to appear at the back of the church with Leandra, and you didn't." His thumbs ran across her knuckles, then he let go of her hands altogether. "I want you to walk down that aisle toward me because that's where you want to be, Tara. Regardless of the baby. Regardless of my family."

She went still. Afraid to move, to breathe.

"I've been in love with you from practically the first time we met." His voice went gruff. "I should have told you. Baby or no baby. Crazy brother of yours or no crazy brother of yours. Nosy family of mine or none. I want to marry you. I'll even give up my job if that's what it takes to prove to you that the life we can have will be different than what you fear."

"Oh, Axel." Everything inside her melted. Not just from the words, but from the naked emotion shining in his golden eyes. She pressed her fingers over his lips. "I do love your family," she whispered. "But I'm in love with *you.* I have been since that weekend in Braden." She sucked in a quick, shaking breath. "I've made my way in this world on my own for a long time. I could have kept on doing it even with our child. That was the safe route. But I don't want that route anymore. I want you." She looked up at him. "I know you're not like my father. I *know* that now and it doesn't matter what you do. You are who you are." She took his hand and pressed it to the fluttering inside her abdomen. "I realized something, too. I don't just want roots, Axel. I want the entire tree." She smiled through her tears. "I want the branches, the buds, the leaves. That's what loving you is like. It's not only a root shooting down to the center of the earth. It's everything else that moves outward. Upward. It's what lifts me."

His eyes gleamed. "I'll plant you an orchard, then."

She laughed brokenly and swiped her wet cheeks. She lifted his hand and pressed her lips to the skin over his knuckles that had healed since he'd broken Ryan's picture. "But I don't want to wait until the church is ready for another wedding. We can get married at the courthouse when it opens on Monday."

"Courthouse?" Squire's voice rang up to them on the landing. "What the hell kind of nonsense is that?"

"Squire," Gloria tried hushing him, but he just planted his gnarled walking stick in front of him and stared at them when they looked down.

"If there's one thing this family oughta be able to do by now is pull a wedding together," he pointed out as if he were the last sensible person on the planet. "Barn's already all set up for the reception, isn't it?"

"That's true," Emily agreed and Tara turned with surprise. She'd forgotten all about Axel's mother standing nearby. "Of course we'll need to do something about your dress." She looked misty-eyed as she tapped her finger against her lips.

"And we'll have to round up Reverend Stone again," Jefferson added from downstairs. Tara realized all the rifles were magically gone again. "At least he's used to the weddings in this family not coming off quite like they're planned."

"And we'll get your brother," Axel added quietly, taking her in his arms as the discussion seemed to take on a life of its own right around them. "Except I'm pretty sure he's not going to want to give you away to me."

She looped her hands around his neck, feeling like her heart might burst right out of her, she felt so full. "There's nothing for him to give. I'm already yours. I have been since you told me to make a wish and blow out the candles on that birthday cake in Braden."

His hands slid up her spine and his mouth hovered over hers. "What'd you wish for?"

"You," she said simply. "I wished for you."

"That was a good wish," he said huskily, and closed his lips over hers.

# *Epilogue*

In the end, it wasn't until that night before Axel and Tara could take their place together in front of Reverend Stone to say their vows.

They'd had to send someone into town to retrieve the marriage license that had been in the pastor's office, which was thankfully untouched by the blaze. But that had entailed both Max and Tristan working around the fire department, who'd deemed the entire facility off limits.

Then there was Sloan and getting him out of the clutches of the ER doctors who'd sewn up the slash in his arm where the bullet had grazed him. Fortunately, Rebecca had some sway when it came to the workings of her own hospital.

And of course there were the dozens of times Axel had to stop what he was doing to explain to yet another person what had transpired in Weaver that afternoon.

Tara, who'd spent a good portion of that time in a bedroom behind the stairs while the women in Axel's family fussed around her, had fairly floated through the hours. The only thing she cared about was Axel.

But finally, the details had all been taken care of, and the only thing left to do was for Tara to dress. All she was waiting for was Leandra, who was going to help her.

But the person who knocked at the bedroom door didn't turn out to be Axel's sister at all. It was Sloan who stuck his head in. "I don't suppose I can talk you out of this?"

She shook her head. Laughed a little. "No."

He grimaced. "Yeah. Well, I just want to get this out before I don't have a chance to." He closed the door on the laughter they could hear drifting through the house. He was wearing a borrowed black jacket over his bandaged arm. "I thought I was doing the right thing. I lost Maria. I didn't want to lose you, too."

"Oh, bean. Axel told me about her. I'm so sorry. I know if he could change what happened—" She shook her head, her hands spreading.

His lips twisted. "Blaming him seemed easier than blaming myself. I told her the truth about me. About you." He shook his head. "She must have told her brother. I never meant to ruin your life, Tara."

Her eyes filled. "What's ruined? I've found what I never thought I'd find. A place in this world."

"Weaver?"

"Beside the man I'm marrying. The man I love," she corrected, letting out a shaky breath. "I never understood before why Mom stayed with Dad. But maybe I'm beginning to." She tugged at his jacket lapel. "I just wish you'd stay for a while."

"I have to get back to Chicago to finish testifying. But after that?" He gave a faint smile that was almost reminiscent of the old Sloan. "I might have to come back and make sure you bring that niece or nephew of mine into the world all right. For now, though, you are going to be a beautiful bride."

"Only if I get dressed first." The gown that Emily, Maggie and Jaimie had furiously wielded their sewing needles over was draped across the bed. It was Gloria who'd unearthed the lace gown that had belonged to Squire's first wife, Sarah. The woman who'd given him his five sons before tragedy had taken her.

"Well." Her brother looked awkward for a moment and she made a face, pulling him into her arms for a hug. He hugged her back. "I'll be in the living room when you're ready," he said, sounding a little hoarse, before leaving the room.

Tara let out a long breath, dashing her hands down the front of the robe that Jaimie had loaned her. She wandered to the French doors that overlooked the rear of the house and peered out. It was dark, but in the distance, she could see the new barn. All lit up, ready and waiting for a wedding reception.

But first, there needed to be a wedding and for that, there needed to be a bride. Preferably one wearing something other than a robe.

She didn't know what was keeping Leandra, but that didn't mean Tara couldn't step into a lace gown on her own. She started to turn to the bed, but a movement outside caught her eye. A man, heading away from the house.

She wasn't sure why she peered harder through the windowpane. Leftover adrenaline. Curiosity. Or maybe just the fact that he seemed familiar. But she did, and just then, he looked back and light from the big house caught him square in the face.

She blinked, too stunned for a moment to react. But then the man turned away again, and she scrabbled with the latch on the French door, finally throwing it open to run out on the deck. "Ryan!"

The figure hesitated for a fraction of a second, only to keep moving.

She gathered the robe around her legs and raced across the

deck. Her slippers nearly came off when she hit the snow, but she didn't stop as she chased after the swiftly moving man. It wasn't just his face that had been familiar. "Wait! Please wait!"

By some miracle, the tall man turned and headed back toward her. "You're nuts," Ryan Clay said bluntly, taking in her robe and slippers.

She caught his sleeve, afraid he'd disappear into the night. "You were outside the church this afternoon," she realized breathlessly. "I thought you were a guest. I'm Tara—"

"I know who you are. I'm just surprised it took Axel five years to get you to the altar."

She blinked at that. "Why are you out here hiding in the shadows?"

His lips twisted. "I shouldn't have come."

"Shouldn't have… Now you're the one who's nuts! Don't you know how happy everyone will be to see you? Why come at all, if not to see your family?"

"You don't even know me." He shook off her hand and headed away.

She shivered. "I know Axel," she said after him. "I know he never gave up on you. And I know only too well that he deserves better than to have to lie to everyone he loves about you."

But her words just seemed to disappear in the snowflakes that drifted in the air.

She blew out a breath, her hands clenching in the robe.

"Tara?"

She whirled. Leandra was standing on the deck, staring after her as if she'd lost her mind.

Maybe she had. Maybe Ryan was a figment of her imagination. A wishful conjuring that could finally put Axel's mind at ease.

She gathered up her robe and picked her way back to the deck.

"You all right?" Leandra followed her inside. "What were

you doing?" She dashed her hands over the few snowflakes on Tara's shoulders.

Tara sighed and managed a smile. "I don't know. Wishing on the stars, I guess."

"For a second I was afraid you were running out on Axel."

At that, Tara's heart settled. "Never."

Leandra studied her for another moment. Whatever she saw must have reassured her, for she relaxed and shook her head wryly. "I think maybe I should have brought you some food when I hit the kitchen a few minutes ago," she murmured. "So let's get you dressed so we can get to the spread over in the barn sometime yet tonight."

Within minutes, the robe was replaced by the gown; the slippers by delicate heels that were thoroughly impractical considering the snow outside. But they were beautiful and Tara couldn't help feeling a little like Cinderella.

Leandra fussed around her for a few minutes then handed her a bouquet. Not the peonies, since they'd perished in the bride's room at the church. "It's sage," she said. "Not exactly roses, but it does smell good."

Tara held the ribbon-bound bouquet to her nose. The stalks did smell good. She also knew the herb signified wisdom which seemed pretty fitting, all things considered.

Leandra handed her the ivory cashmere cloak that had been a contribution from Axel's Aunt Maggie. "I'll go out and get the ball rolling." She winked and Tara swung the cloak around her shoulders before following her out to the living room where Sloan was waiting.

"I knew you'd be beautiful," he said, tucking her arm through his and heading for the front door. "But only Wyoming folk would think nothing of putting on a wedding outside on a March night. You know it's snowing, right?"

"I think it's perfect," she assured him as they stepped out onto the porch.

She sucked in a breath of delight at the sight that awaited across the circular drive.

Tiny white lights were strung through the trees, twinkling against the gentle drift of snowflakes that fell on the family gathered there.

Her family now, too.

Then when she and Sloan crossed the drive, the sweet strains of a violin filled the air. Casey, she realized with some surprise, spotting him off to one side with the instrument.

Reverend Stone was standing at the head of the impromptu aisle where Leandra and Evan were already waiting.

And then the only one Tara had eyes for was Axel as her brother escorted her across the snow toward him.

The torn gray suit and tie he'd worn at the church had been replaced by a dark blazer over a collarless shirt. It wasn't traditional. But it was oh-so-perfect for him.

And when she stopped next to him, he closed his warm hands around hers and his slow smile that was just for her could have stolen her heart if she hadn't already given it to him.

Reverend Stone cleared his throat slightly. "Who gives this woman to this man?"

Sloan stepped forward again. "I guess that'd be me."

A few chuckles sounded at that. Her brother looked hesitant for a moment, then dropped a kiss on her cheek and stepped away again.

The minister looked pleased. "Marriage is an honorable estate," he began. "Not to be entered into unadvisedly, but reverently and—"

"Impatiently," Axel murmured into her ear.

She buried her smile in the bouquet of sage.

But when it came time to say "I do," their voices rang true and serious. And when Reverend Stone finally got to the part where the groom could sweetly kiss the bride, cheers sounded through the night.

There was no chance for a walk back down the aisle with her brand new husband then, because the family simply descended on them with hugs and kisses and a great deal of laughter.

"D'ya think we might be smart enough to get outta the snow?" Squire's complaint carried above the celebrating. "I'm an old man. This ain't good for me."

"You're an old man who wants to get to that wedding cake that's been waiting all day in the barn," Jefferson drawled. His arms were looped around his wife's waist.

"Smart-aleck son," Squire grumbled, stomping the tip of his cane into the snow. "Don't know where the hell you get it from."

"From you," Tara said, then bit her lip in the sudden silence that followed as Squire moved closer to her. She almost quailed as his crafty gaze ran her up and down.

"Guess you'd be right about that," he finally agreed. "That dress belonged to Axel's grandma, you know."

She looked down at the yards of lace. She did know. Which had made it so very special. "Do you mind?" Gloria had promised that he wouldn't.

His eyes narrowed even more. "You look right nice, actually. My Sarah would've been pleased to see it. And it's true. The only thing I mind right now is waiting around for that cake. It's chocolate, I'm told." He thumped his cane again. "So let's get to it!"

And so they did. Some of them loaded up in vehicles to drive the short distance. Some just headed out across the field, despite the snow on the ground and in the air.

Axel simply swept Tara up in his arms, making her heart dance. "Can't have your feet getting any colder in those shoes," he murmured.

She looped her hands around his shoulders. Happiness was a bubble inside her, ready to burst. "It's going to take a miracle, you know, if you intend on carrying me—us—all the way to the barn."

Axel's gaze met hers and the love that was there was enough to spend a lifetime savoring. Cherishing. "You and our baby are the only miracles I need." His lips covered hers in a long, long kiss.

Then he lifted his head and continued carrying her, walking right across the field in the wake of the others who'd gone ahead of them.

She tilted her head back, blinking at the snowflakes that drifted into her face. This. This was her place. In the arms of the man she loved.

She lifted her head again to savor the sight of her husband's face, and caught a glimpse of a man behind them.

Not moving into the shadows. But out of them.

Toward them.

She smiled and pressed her cheek against Axel's broad shoulder. "Oh, my love," she whispered, "I think there is still room tonight for another miracle...."

* * * * *

"I'm the illegitimate daughter of notoriously scandalous parents, Mr. Milford. Candidates for my hand are unlikely to be lining up at the gates."

"Don't be so quick to discount your charms, my dear. Or the charm of your substantial dowry. Or even your brothers' influence. There are as many reasons to marry as there are marriages."

Annalise snorted. "Oh, yes. Perhaps I shall marry for dynastic reasons, or perhaps for property or influence. After all, a loveless, practical marriage worked out so well for my mother."

"Well, you've routed me on that one. I can think of no suitable rejoinder." Ned rose to his feet and extended his hand. "And since that is the case, let me be the first to wish you a long and happy spinsterhood."

Her mouth gaped open. And then she laughed.

And he froze.

This was the first time, Ned realized. The first time he'd

seen her eyes light up and her mouth curl. The first time he'd witnessed her features melded together in glorious accord to produce exquisite beauty.

Unbelievable what a change came over her face. Unheard of what effect her throaty, rasping laughter had on his body. It pounded a beat upon his ear, quickly taken up by his pulse. It echoed through him, finally residing in his stirring nether regions.

So easily she did it, awakened these sensations within him—without any apparent effort at all. And she had called him potentially dangerous? Clearly the intelligent thing for him to do would be to steer clear, to leave her to the tender ministrations of Lord Peter Blackthorne.

"You were right." She smiled up at him as she took his hand and climbed to her feet. "I do feel better."

Ah, well. When had he ever chosen the intelligent path?

He did not relinquish her hand. He used it to pull her in, close enough that he could feel the warmth of her. "At the risk of repeating Lord Peter's mistake and anticipating too much—may I ask if you'll be my partner in battledore tomorrow?"

Her smiled dimmed. Her breath came a little faster. His own had gone shallow, as if he'd just run a race—and lost. He ran his gaze over the appealing lift of her brow and the curious angle of her chin. His index finger twitched.

"I should like that," she said.

His finger trembled again and he lifted it, traced the pink and tender shell of her ear, the unique sweep of her jaw. Her pulse leaped beneath her skin, triggering his own. Slowly he tilted her chin up, waiting for her to object, to step back, to slap his hand away.

She did none of those eminently sensible things. Which left him free to do the entirely impractical thing.

Baby soft, the skin of her lips. Her whole body trembled when he touched her there.

He leaned in. Her eyes closed, even as she stood straight against him, strung as tight as a bow. He pressed his mouth to hers. It was a soft kiss, sweet and chaste. And yet he was hot and hard and as ready as he'd ever been in his life.

She drew back a little. Sighed. Their breath mingled a moment before she slowly backed away.

"Oh," she breathed. Her dark eyes were full of wonder and something that looked like fear. He took a step toward her, but she only shook her head. His outstretched hand fell to his side as she turned to disappear into the wood. This was the first time, Ned realized. The first time, since he'd come to the house party at Welbourne Manor, that he'd seen her eyes light up.

* * * * *